Penguin Books
A Kestrel for a Knave

Barry Hines was born in 1939 at the mining village of Hyland Common, near Barnsley, where his father worked down the pit. Educated at Ecclesfield Grammar School, he achieved the honour of being selected to play for the England Grammar Schools' soccer team. On leaving school it was perhaps a natural, though temporary, step to play football for Barnsley, mainly in their 'A' team, while also working variously as an apprentice mining surveyor, a labourer mending hydraulic pit props, and as an assistant in a blacksmith's shop. Following this interlude, he entered Loughborough Training College where he studied Physical Education for three years. On the completion of his course there, he came south to London where for two years he taught physical education in a comprehensive school. Barry Hines, who has now returned to the North, is married and has one child. His first novel, *The Blinder*, was published in Penguin in 1969. His latest book is *The Gamekeeper* (1975).

Barry Hines

A Kestrel for a Knave

Penguin Books

Penguin Books Ltd, Harmondsworth,
Middlesex, England
Penguin Books, 625 Madison Avenue,
New York, New York 10022, U.S.A.
Penguin Books Australia Ltd, Ringwood,
Victoria, Australia
Penguin Books Canada Ltd, 2801 John Street,
Markham, Ontario, Canada L3R 1B4
Penguin Books (N.Z.) Ltd, 182-190 Wairau Road,
Auckland 10, New Zealand

First published by Michael Joseph 1968
Published in Penguin Books 1969
Reprinted 1970 (twice), 1971, 1972 (twice), 1973 (twice),
1974 (three times), 1975 (twice), 1976 (twice), 1977, 1978, 1979

Made and printed in Great Britain by
Hazell Watson & Viney Ltd,
Aylesbury, Bucks
Set in Linotype Pilgrim

To Richard

'An Eagle for an Emperor, a Gyrfalcon for a King; a
Peregrine for a Prince, a Saker for a Knight, a Merlin
for a Lady; a Goshawk for a Yeoman, a Sparrowhawk
for a Priest, a Musket for a Holy water Clerk, a
Kestrel for a Knave.'

Selected from the Boke of St Albans, 1486,
and a Harleian manuscript.

There were no curtains up. The window was a hard edged block the colour of the night sky. Inside the bedroom the darkness was of a gritty texture. The wardrobe and bed were blurred shapes in the darkness. Silence.

Billy moved over, towards the outside of the bed. Jud moved with him, leaving one half of the bed empty. He snorted and rubbed his nose. Billy whimpered. They settled. Wind whipped the window and swept along the wall outside.

Billy turned over. Jud followed him and cough-coughed into his neck. Billy pulled the blankets up round his ears and wiped his neck with them. Most of the bed was now empty, and the unoccupied space quickly cooled. Silence. Then the alarm rang. The noise brought Billy upright, feeling for it in the darkness, eyes shut tight. Jud groaned and hutched back across the cold sheet. He reached down the side of the bed and knocked the clock over, grabbed for it, and knocked it farther away.

'Come here, you bloody thing.'

He stretched down and grabbed it with both hands. The glass lay curved in one palm, while the fingers of his other hand fumbled amongst the knobs and levers at the back. He found the lever and the noise stopped. Then he coiled back into bed and left the clock lying on its back.

'The bloody thing.'

He stayed in his own half of the bed, groaning and turning over every few minutes, Billy lay with his back to him, listening. Then he turned his cheek slightly from the pillow.

'Jud?'

'What?'

'Tha'd better get up.'

No answer.

'Alarm's gone off tha knows.'

'Think I don't know?'

He pulled the blankets tighter and drilled his head into the pillow. They both lay still.

'Jud?'

'What?'

'Tha'll be late.'

'O, shut it.'

'Clock's not fast tha knows.'

'I said S H U T I T.'

He swung his fist under the blankets and thumped Billy in the kidneys.

'Gi'o'er! That hurts!'

'Well shut it then.'

'I'll tell my mam on thi.'

Jud swung again. Billy scuffled away into the cold at the edge of the bed, sobbing. Jud got out, sat on the edge of the bed for a moment, then stood up and felt his way across the room to the light switch. Billy worked his way back to the centre and disappeared under the blankets.

'Set t'alarm for me, Jud. For seven.'

'Set it thi sen.'

'Go on, thar up.'

Jud parted Billy's sweater and shirt, and used the sweater for a vest. Billy snuggled down in Jud's place, making the springs creak. Jud looked at the humped blankets, then walked across and pulled them back, stripping the bed completely.

'Hands off cocks; on socks.'

For an instant Billy lay curled up, his hands wafered between his thighs. Then he sat up and crawled to the bottom of the bed to retrieve the blankets.

'You rotten sod, just because tha's to get up.'

'Another few weeks lad, an' tha'll be getting up wi' me.'

He walked out on to the landing. Billy propped himself up on one elbow.

'Switch t'light out, then!'

Jud went downstairs. Billy sat on the edge of the bed and

re-set the alarm, then ran across the lino and switched the light off. When he got back into bed most of the warmth had gone. He shivered and scuffled around the sheet, seeking a warm place.

It was still dark outside when he got up and went downstairs. The living-room curtains were drawn, and when he switched the light on it was gloomy and cold without the help of the fire. He placed the clock on the mantelpiece, then picked up his mother's sweater from the settee and pulled it on over his shirt.

The alarm rang as he was emptying the ashes in the dustbin. Dust clouded up into his face as he dropped the lid back on and ran inside, but the noise stopped before he could reach it. He knelt down in front of the empty grate and scrunched sheets of newspaper into loose balls, arranging them in the grate like a bouquet of hydrangea flowers. Then he picked up the hatchet, stood a nog of wood on the hearth and struck it down the centre. The blade bit and held. He lifted the hatchet with the nog attached and smashed it down, splitting the nog in half and chipping the tile with the blade. He split the halves into quarters down through eighths to sixteenths, then arranged these sticks over the paper like the struts of a wigwam. He completed the construction with lumps of coal, building them into a loose shell, so that sticks and paper showed through the chinks. The paper caught with the first match, and the flames spread quickly underneath, making the chinks smoke and the sticks crack. He waited for the first burst of flames up the back of the construction, then stood up and walked into the kitchen, and opened the pantry door. There were a packet of dried peas and a half bottle of vinegar on the shelves. The bread bin was empty. Just inside the doorway, the disc of the electricity meter circled slowly in its glass case. The red arrow appeared, and disappeared. Billy closed the door and opened the outside door. On the step stood two empty milk bottles. He thumped the jamb with the side of his fist.

'It's t' same every morning. I'm going to start hiding some at nights.'

9

He started to turn inside, then stopped, and looked out again. The garage door was open. He ran across the concrete strip and used the light from the kitchen to look inside.

'Well, of all the rotten tricks!'

He kicked a can of oil the length of the garage and ran back into the house. The coal had caught fire, and the yellow flames were now emitting a slight warmth. Billy pulled his pumps on without unfastening the laces and grabbed his windcheater. The zip was broken and the material draped out behind him as he vaulted the front wall and raced up the avenue.

The sky was a grey wash; pale grey over the fields behind the estate, but darkening overhead, to charcoal away over the city. The street lamps were still on and a few lighted windows glowed the colours of their curtains. Billy passed two miners returning silently from the night shift. A man in overalls cycled by, treading the pedals slowly. The four of them converged, and parted, pursuing their various destinations at various speeds.

Billy reached the recreation ground. The gate was locked, so he stepped back and sprang on to the interlaced wire fence, scaled it and placed one foot on top ready for the descent. The whole section between the concrete posts shuddered beneath his weight. He rode it, with one hand and one foot on top, the other arm fighting for balance; but the more he fought, the more it shook, until finally it shook him off, over the other side into the long grass. He stood up. His pumps and jeans were saturated, and there was dog shit on one hand. He wiped it in the grass, smelled his fingers, then ran across the football pitch. Behind the top goal, the rows of children's swings had all been wrapped round their horizontal supporting bars. He found a dog-hole in the fence at the other side of the pitch and crept through on to the City Road. A double-decker bus passed, followed closely by two cars. Their engines faded and no other vehicles approached. The road lamps went out, and for a few moments the only sound in the dark morning was the squelch of Billy's pumps as he crossed the road.

A bell tinkled as he entered the shop. Mr Porter glanced up, then continued to arrange newspapers into overlapping rows on the counter.

'I thought you weren't coming.'

'Why, I'm not late, am I?'

Porter pulled a watch out of his waistcoat pocket and held it in his palm like a stopwatch. He considered it, then tucked it away. Billy picked up the canvas bag from the front of the counter and ducked under the strap as he slipped it over his head and shoulder. The bag sagged at his hip. He straightened a twist in the strap, then lifted the flap and looked inside at the wad of newspapers and magazines.

'I nearly wa' though.'

'What do you mean?'

'Late. Our Jud went to t'pit on my bike.'

Porter stopped sorting and looked across the counter.

'What you going to do, then?'

'Walk it.'

'Walk it! And how long do you think that's going to take you?'

'It'll not take me long.'

'Some folks like to read their papers t'day they come out, you know.'

'It's not my fault. I didn't ask him to take it, did I?'

'No, and I didn't ask for any cheek from you! Do you hear?'

Billy heard.

''Cos there's a waiting list a mile long for your job, you know. Grand lads an' all, some of 'em. Lads from up Firs Hill and round there.'

Billy shuffled his feet and glanced down into the bag, as though one of the grand lads might be waiting in there.

'It'll not take me that much longer. I've done it before.'

Porter shook his head and squared off a pile of magazines by tapping their four edges on the counter. Billy sidled across to the convector heater and stood before it, feet apart, hands behind his back. Porter looked up at him and Billy let his hands fall to his sides.

'I don't know, it's typical.'

'What's up, I haven't let you down yet, have I?'

The bell tinkled. Porter straightened up, smiling.

'Morning, Sir. Not very promising again.'

'Twenty Players.'

'Right, Sir.'

He turned round and ran one finger along a shelf stacked with cigarettes. His finger reached the Players and climbed the packets. Billy reached out and lifted two bars of chocolate from a display table at the side of the counter. He dropped them into his bag as Porter turned round. Porter traded the cigarettes and sprang the till open.

'Than-kyou,' his last syllable rising, in time to the ring of the bell.

'Good morning, Sir.'

He watched the man out of the shop, then turned back to Billy.

'You know what they said when I took you on, don't you?'

He waited, as though expecting Billy to supply the answer.

'They said, you'll have to keep your eyes open now, you know, 'cos they're all alike off that estate. They'll take your breath if you're not careful.'

'I've never taken owt o' yours, have I?'

'I've never given you chance, that's why.'

'You don't have to. I've stopped getting into trouble now.'

Porter opened his mouth, blinked, then pulled his watch out and studied the time.

'Are you going to stand there all day, then?'

He shook the watch and placed it to one ear.

'Next thing I know, everybody'll be ringing me up and asking why I can't deliver on time.'

Billy left the shop. The traffic was now continuous along the City Road, and there were queues at all the bus stops for buses into town. Billy passed them as he headed away from the city. He started to deliver at a row of detached houses and bungalows: pebble-dash and stone, and leaded windows. The row ended and he turned off the main road, up Firs Hill. The hill was steep. Trees had been planted at regular intervals along a cropped verge and the houses stood well back, shielded from the road, and from each other by trees and high wicker fences. Billy stopped before a wrought-iron gate with spikes at the top. On one of the gate posts was a notice: NO HAWKERS NO CALLERS. Billy looked down the drive and popped two squares of chocolate into his mouth. He left one half of the gate wide open and set off towards the house. Rhododendron shrubs crowded both sides of the drive, right up to the front door. He pushed the flap. It was stiff and the spring creaked. He looked towards the corners of the house, then eased the paper through and slowly lowered the flap until it clamped the paper. The curtains in all the front windows were drawn. The garden was wild, and moss and grass were replacing the asphalt on the drive. Billy used the moss and the grass like stepping stones until the last few yards, then he sprinted out, slamming the gate shut behind him. He unwrapped the last two squares of chocolate and looked back. A thrush ran out from under a rhododendron shrub and started to tug a worm from the soil between the loose asphalt chips. It stood over the worm and tugged vertically, exposing its speckled throat and pointing its beak to the sky. The worm stretched, but held. The thrush lowered its head and backed off, pulling at a more acute angle. The worm still held, so the thrush stepped in and jerked at the slack. The worm ripped out of the ground and the thrush ran away with it, back under the shrubs. Billy flicked the chocolate wrapper through the gate and passed on.

A milk dray whined up the hill, close to the kerb. Every time the near wheels dipped into a grate, the bottles rattled in their crates. It stopped and the driver jumped out of the cab whistling. He slid a crate off the back and carried it across the road. Billy glanced round as he approached the dray. There was no one else on the hill. He lifted a bottle of orange juice and a carton of eggs and popped them into his bag. When the driver returned, Billy was delivering papers at the next house. The dray passed him again further up. It stopped and the driver lit a cigarette, waiting for Billy to draw level.

'How's it going then, young un?'

Billy stopped and lolled back against the dray.

'O, not so bad.'

'Tha could do wi' some transport.'

He grinned and patted the dray.

'This is better than walking, tha knows.'

'Ar, only just, though.'

Billy kicked the back tyre.

'They only go about five miles an hour, these things.'

'It's still better than walking, isn't it?'

'I could go faster on a kid's scooter.'

The milkman nipped his cigarette out and blew on the end.

'You know what I always say?'

'What?'

'Third class riding's better than first class walking anyday.'

He tucked the tab into the breast pocket of his overalls and crossed the road, carrying two bottles in each hand. Billy watched him across the open back of the dray, then dipped into his bag for the orange. He held the bottle horizontally between thumb and little finger, then tilted it to make the air bubble travel the length of the bottle, and back again. Top to bottom, top bottom to bottom, until the flakes raged like a glass snow storm. He punched his thumb through the cap, and downed the contents in two gulps, dropped the bottle back into a crate, and passed on up the hill.

A lane cut across the top of Firs Hill, forming a T junction. Billy turned left along it. There was no pavement, and whenever a car approached he either crossed the lane or stepped into the long grass at the side and waited for it to pass. Fields, and a few hedgerow trees sloped down into the valley. Toy traffic travelled along the City Road, and across the road, in the valley bottom, was the sprawl of the estate. Towards the city, a pit chimney and the pit-head winding gear showed above the rooftops, and at the back of the estate was a patchwork of fields, black, and grey, and pale winter green; giving way to a wood, which stood out on the far slope as clear as an ink blot.

Billy pulled his jacket together as the wind murmured over the top of the moor, and across into the lane. But the zip was broken and the jacket fell open again. He crossed the lane and crouched down with his back against the wall. The stones were

wet, and shone different shades of brown and green, like
polished leather. Billy opened his bag and flicked through the
contents. He pulled out the *Dandy* and turned immediately to
Desperate Dan.

Dan is going to a wedding. His nephew and niece are helping
him to get ready. His niece puts his top hat on the chair.
Crunch! goes that hat as Dan sits on it. He goes to buy a new
hat, but they are all FAR TOO SMALL. This is the biggest in
the shop, the assistant tells him. Dan tries it on. It's almost big
enough he says, but when he tries to pull it down a bit, he rips
the brim off and it comes down over his face. *OH, NO!* he
says, looking over the brim. Outside the shop he has an idea,
and points to something not shown in the picture. *Ah! That's
the very thing!* he says, but first he has to clear the City Square
so that no one will see what he is going to do. Round the corner,
he bends over a water hydrant and blows. Water explodes out
of the fountain in the square, drenching everybody, and they
all have to go home, leaving the square deserted. Good, now I
can get what I want, Dan says. In the next picture, Dan is trying on a big grey topper. He looks pleased and says, *That's it!
And it fits a treat.* He attends the wedding, and at the Recep-
tion Hall he hands his hat to the cloakroom attendant. The
attendant can't hold it and the hat goes *Crunch!* on his foot.
Ooyah! goes the attendant. He tries to pick it up, saying, *Help!
What a hat! It's made of solid stone!* The last picture shows
where the hat came from: from the head of the statue in the
City Square: WILLIAM SMITH, MAYOR OF CACTUS-
VILLE 1865–86. SHOT AT HIGH NOON BY BLACK JAKE.

Billy stood up into the wind and flexed his knees as he stepped back on to the lane. He started to run, holding the bag
under one arm to stop it slapping and dragging at his hip. He
delivered the *Dandy* with a newspaper and several magazines
at a farmhouse. A collie barked at his heels all the way through
the yard, and back out again. It followed him along the lane,
then stopped and barked him out of sight over a rise. Billy
started to run again. He rolled a newspaper into a telescope
and spied through it as he ran. Until he spied a stone house,
standing back from the lane. Then he slowed to a walk, smooth-

ing out the newspaper and rolling it the other way to neutralize the first curve.

At the side of the house, a grey Bentley was parked before an open garage. Billy never took his eyes off it as he walked up the drive, and when he reached the top, he veered across and looked in at the dashboard. The front door of the house opened, making him step back quickly from the car and turn round. A man in a dark suit came out, followed by two little girls in school uniform. They all climbed into the front of the car, and the little girls waved to a woman in a dressing gown standing at the door. Billy handed her the newspaper and looked past her into the house. The hall and stairs were carpeted. A radiator with a glass shelf ran along one wall, and on the shelf stood a vase of fresh daffodils. The car freewheeled down the drive and turned into the lane. The woman waved with the newspaper and closed the door. Billy walked back, pushed the letter box up and peeped through. There was the sound of running bath water. A radio was playing. The woman was walking up the stairs, carrying a transistor. Billy lowered the flap and walked away. On the drive the tyres of the car had imprinted two patterned bands, reminiscent of markings on a snake's back.

Outside the shop, Billy transferred the carton of eggs from the delivery bag to a large pocket, sewn into the lining of his jacket. The pocket pouched under the weight, but when he closed his jacket, there was no bulge on the outside.

Porter looked round at the sound of the bell. He was up a step ladder behind the counter, re-lining shelves with fresh paper.

'Evening.'

'I told you it wouldn't take me long, didn't I?'

'What did you do, throw half of 'em over a hedge?'

'No need. I know some short cuts coming back.'

'I'll bet you do, over people's property, no doubt.'

'No, across some fields. It cuts miles off.'

'It's a good job t'farmer didn't see you, else you might have got a barrel of shotspread up your arse.'

'What for? There was only grass in 'em.'

Billy folded the bag in half and placed it on the counter.

'Not on there. You know where it goes.'

Billy walked round the counter and squeezed past the step ladder. Porter hung on until he had passed, then he watched him open a drawer at the back of the counter and stuff the bag inside.

'You'll be wanting me to take 'em round for you next.'

Billy shut the drawer with his knee and looked up at him.

'What time is it?'

'It's time you were at school.'

'It's not that late, is it?'

Porter turned back to the shelves, shaking his head slowly.

'I shouldn't like to think it wa' my job trying to learn you owt.'

As Billy squeezed past, he shook the steps and grabbed Porter's legs.

'Look out, Mr Porter!'

Porter sprawled forward into the shelving, his arms spread wide, his fingers scratching for a hold.

'You're all right, I've got you!'

Billy held Porter's legs while he pushed himself off the shelves and regained his balance. His face and bald patch were greasy with sweat.

'You clumsy young bugger. What you trying to do, kill me?'

'I lost my balance.'

'I wouldn't put it past you, either.'

He descended the steps backwards, holding on with both hands.

'I fair felt my heart go then.'

He reached the bottom of the steps and placed one hand over the breast pocket of his jacket. Reassured, he sat down on the stool behind the counter and exhaled noisily.

'Are you all right now, Mr Porter?'

'All right! Ar, I'm bloody champion!'

'I'll be off then.'

He crossed the shop to the door.

'And don't be late tonight.'

The estate was teeming with children: tots hand in hand with their mothers, tots on their own, and with other tots, groups of tots and Primary School children; Secondary School children, on their own, in pairs and in threes, in gangs and on bikes. Walking silently, walking on walls, walking and talking, quietly, loudly, laughing; running, chasing, playing, swearing, smoking, ringing bells and calling names: all on their way to school.

When Billy arrived home, the curtains were still drawn in all the front windows, but the light was on in the living-room. As he crossed the front garden, a man appeared from round the side of the house and walked up the path to the gate. Billy watched him walk away down the avenue, then ran round to the back door and into the kitchen.

'Is that you, Reg?'

Billy banged the door and walked through into the living-room. His mother was standing in her underslip, a lipstick poised at her mouth, watching the doorway through the mirror. When she saw Billy, she started to apply the lipstick.

'O, it's you, Billy. Haven't you gone to school yet?'

'Who's that bloke?'

His mother pressed her lips together and stood the capsule, like a bullet, on the mantelpiece.

'That's Reg. You know Reg, don't you?'

She took a cigarette packet from the mantelpiece and shook it.

'Hell! I forgot to ask him for one.'

She dropped the packet into the hearth and turned to Billy.

'You haven't got a fag on you, have you, love?'

Billy moved across to the table and placed both hands round the teapot. His mother pulled her skirt on and tried to zip it on the hip. The zip would only close half-way, so she secured the waistband with a safety pin. The zip slipped as soon as she moved, and the slit expanded to the shape of a rugby ball. Billy shoved a finger down the spout of the teapot.

'Is that him you come home wi' last night?'

'There's some tea mashed if you want a cup, but I don't know if t'milk's come or not.'

'Was it?'

'Oh, stop pestering me! I'm late enough as it is.'

She crumpled her sweater into a tyre and eased her head through the hole, trying to prevent her hair from touching the sides.

'Do me a favour, love, and run up to t'shop for some fags.'

'They'll not be open yet.'

'You can go to t'back door. Mr Hardy'll not mind.'

'I can't, I'll be late.'

'Go on, love, and bring a few things back wi' you; a loaf and some butter, and a few eggs, summat like that.'

'Go your sen.'

'I've not time. Just tell him to put it in t'book and I'll pay him at t'week-end.'

'He says you can't have owt else 'til you've paid up.'

'He always says that. I'll give you a tanner if you go.'

'I don't want a tanner. I'm off now.'

He moved towards the door, but his mother stepped across and blocked his way.

'Billy, get up to that shop and do as you're telled.'

He shook his head. His mother stepped forward, but he backed off, keeping the same distance between them. Although she was too far away, she still swiped at him, and although he saw her hand coming, and going, well clear of his face, he still flicked his head back instinctively.

'I'm not going.'

He moved behind the table.

'Aren't you? We'll see about that.'

They faced each other across the table, their fingers spread on the cloth, like two pianists ready to begin.

'We'll see whether you're going or not, you cheeky young bugger.'

Billy moved to his right. His mother to her left. He stood out from the corner, so that only the length of one side separated them. His mother grabbed for him. Billy shot across the back of the table and round the other corner, but his mother was back in position, waiting. She lunged forward, Billy skipped back and they faced up again from their original positions.

'I'll bloody murder you when I get hold of you.'

'Gi'o'er now, mam, I'll be late for school.'

'You'll be more than late, unless you do as you're telled.'

'He said I'd get t'stick next time.'

'That's nowt to what you'll get if I catch you.'

Billy ducked down. His mother followed, holding on to the table top to retain balance. They faced each other under the table, then Billy feinted a move forward. His mother dived, at nothing. Billy jumped up and ran round the table while his mother was still full stretch on the floor.

'Billy come back! Do you hear? I said come back!'

He whipped the kitchen door open and ran out into the garden. He was half-way down the path when his mother appeared, panting and jabbing her finger at him.

'Just you wait lad! Just you wait 'til tonight!'

She went back in and banged the door. Billy turned away and looked down the garden, over the fence into the fields. A skylark flew up, trilling as it climbed. Higher and higher, until it was just a song in the sky. He opened his jacket and dipped into the pocket. The egg carton was dented. He opened it. Two of the compartments were filled with yellow slime and shell. He eased out the sound eggs and placed them together on the path. Their shells were sticky, so he carefully wiped each one in turn and regrouped them like a four egger, crouching over them and looking down. Then he picked one up, weighed it in his palm, and threw it high in the direction of the house. The egg described a parabola in the air and fell on to the slates. He threw the others in rapid succession, stooping and releasing while the previous one was still in the air. The kitchen door opened and his mother came out. Billy backed away down the path, massaging his right biceps with his left hand. She locked the door and turned round.

'Don't think I've forgotten, lad, 'cos I haven't!'

She slipped the key under the lip of the step, then pulled the ends of her headscarf tight under her chin.

'An' there's a bet of our Jud's to take, an' all. You'd better not forget that.'

'I'm not taking it.'

'You'd better, lad.'

'I'm fed up o' taking 'em. He can take it his sen.'

'How can he, you dozy bugger, if he don't get home in time?'

'I don't care, I'm not taking it.'

'Please yourself then. ...'

She rounded the house and hurried up the path. Billy gave the path a V sign and made a farting noise with his mouth. When he heard the gate bang, he turned round and walked down the path towards a shed at the bottom of the garden. In front of the shed a small square of ground had been covered with pebbles and bordered with whitewashed bricks, set into the soil side by side, at an angle. The roof and sides of the shed had been patched neatly with lengths of tarpaulin. The door had been freshly painted, and a square had been sawn out of the top half and barred vertically with clean laths. On a shelf behind the bars stood a kestrel hawk:

Rufous brown. Flecked breast, dark bars across her back and wings. Wings pointed, crossed over her rump and barred tail. Billy clicked his tongue, and chanted softly, 'Kes, Kes, Kes, Kes.' The hawk looked at him and listened, her fine head held high on strong shoulders, her brown eyes round and alert.

'Did you hear her, Kes, making her mouth again? ... Gooby old cow. Do this, do that, I've to do everything in this house. ... Well they can shit. I'm fed up o' being chased about. ... There's allus somebody after me.'

He slowly lifted one hand and began to rub one of the laths with his forefinger. The hawk watched it all the time.

'An' our Jud, he's t'worst o't'lot, he's allus after me ... allus has been. Like that day last summer when I fetched you, he was after me then. ...'

... Jud was having his breakfast when Billy came downstairs. He glanced up at the clock, It was twenty-five to six.

'What's up wi' thee; shit t'bed?'

'I'm off out, nesting; wi' Tibby and Mac.'

He whooshed the curtains open and switched the light off. The morning light came in as clean as water, making them both look towards the window. The sun had not yet risen, but already the air was warm, and above the roof line of the house opposite, the chimney stack was silhouetted against a cloudless sky.

'It's a smashing morning again.'

'Tha wouldn't be saying that if tha wa' goin' where I'm goin'.'

He poured himself another cup of tea. Billy watched the last dribbles leaving the spout, then put a match to the gas. The kettle began to rumble immediately.

'Just think, when we're goin' up to t'woods, tha'll be goin' down in t'cage.'

'Ar, just think; an' next year tha'll be coming down wi' me.'

'I'll not.'

'Won't tha?'

'No, 'cos I'm not goin' to work down t'pit.'

'Where are tha goin' to work, then?'

Billy poured the boiling water on to the stained leaves in the pot.

'I don't know; but I'm not goin' to work down t'pit.'

'No, and have I to tell thi why? ...'

He walked into the kitchen and came back carrying his jacket.

'... For one thing, tha's to be able to read and write before they'll set thi on. And for another, they wouldn't have a weedy little twat like thee.'

He put his jacket on and went out. Billy poured himself a cup of tea. Jud's snap was still on the table, wrapped up in a cut bread wrapper. Billy turned it round and round with his fingers, sipping his tea. He poured himself another cup, then unwrapped the package and started on the sandwiches.

The kitchen door banged open and Jud rushed through, panting.

'I've forgot my snap.'

He looked at the unwrapped package, and then at Billy, who was holding the ragged half of a sandwich. Billy bolted it into his mouth, slid off his chair and turned it over as Jud came for him. Jud ran into the chair and sprawled full length across it. Billy ran past him, out into the garden and over the fence into the field. A few seconds later, Jud emerged, wrapping up the remainder of his snap. He used it to point at Billy.

'I'll bloody murder thee when I get home!'

Then he pushed it into his jacket pocket and hurried off round the house end. Billy climbed on to the fence and looked round at the sky.

By the time he had crossed the estate and reached Tibby's house, the sun was rising behind a band of cloud, low in the East. High in the sky the moon was still visible, flimsy, and fading as the sun climbed steadily, illuminating the cloud. Until finally the sun appeared, burning the cloud golden, and the moon disappeared in the lightening and warming of the whole sky.

Billy walked round the house, looking up at the drawn curtains. He tried the kitchen door, then stepped back and whispered loudly up at the bedroom window.

'Tibby. Tibby.'

The curtains remained closed. He searched about on the concrete, then picked up a clod of earth from the garden. The crust was damp from the dew, but when he crushed it, the inside was dry and crumbly, and dust puffed up from his palm. He stepped close to the house and lobbed it underhand at the bedroom window. The soil smattered the panes, then fell to the sill, which threw it back to the concrete in a wide arc, like a projection half-way down a waterfall. Down into Billy's face. He ducked his head, spitting and wiping his mouth, then looked up and opened his eyes. The right eye blink-blinked and began to water. He rubbed it with his knuckles but it only reddened the white, and the eye still watered. So he tweezed the lashes between his finger and thumb and drew the lid down, blinking underneath it and looking up at the window with his other eye. The curtains remained closed. He released his eyelid. It blinked once, twice; then stayed up.

At Mac's he used tiny pebbles, pinking them individually off the glass. Pink. Pink. Pink. He had used half a fistful before the curtains were lifted and Mrs MacDowall looked down, clutching

23

her nightdress to her throat. She waved Billy away, but he looked up at her and mouthed,

'Is he up?'

She pushed the window open and leaned out.

'Whadyou want at this time?'

'Is your Mac up?'

"Course he's not up. Do you know what time it is?'

'Isn't he getting up?'

'Not that I know of. He's fast asleep.'

'He's a right 'un. It wa' him that planned it, an' all.'

'Stop shouting, then. Do you want all t'neighbourhood up?'

'He's not coming, then?'

'No, he's not. You'd better come back after breakfast if you want to see him.'

She closed the windows and the curtains fell back into place. Billy scrunched the pebbles round in his fist and looked up at the pane. He threw them, and was running before the first one struck the glass.

He ran back across the estate and straight down the avenue, slowing to a walk as he reached the cul-de-sac, round like the bulb of a thermometer. He cut down a snicket between two houses, out into the fields, leaving the estate behind him.

The sun was up and the cloud band in the East had thinned to a line on the horizon, leaving the dome of the sky clear. The air was still and clean, and the trilling of larks carried far over the fields of hay, which stretched away on both sides of the path. Great rashes of buttercups spread across the fields, and amongst the mingling shades of yellow and green, dog daisies showed their white faces, contrasting with the rust of sorrel. All underscored by clovers, white and pink and purple, which came into their own on the path sides where the grass was shorter, along with daisies and the ubiquitous plantains.

A cushion of mist lay over the fields. Dew drenched the grass, and the occasional sparkling of individual drops made Billy glance down as he passed. One tuft was a silver fire. He knelt down to trace the source of light. The drop had almost forced the blade of grass to the earth, and it lay in the curve of the blade like the tiny egg of a mythical bird. Billy moved his head from side to side to make it sparkle, and when it caught the sun it exploded, throwing out silver needles and crystal splinters. He lowered his head and slowly, very carefully, touched it with the tip of his tongue. The drop quivered like mercury, but held. He bent, and touched it again. It disintegrated and streamed down the channel of the blade to the earth. Slowly the blade began to straighten, climbing steadily like the finger of a clock.

Billy stood up and walked on. He climbed over a stile and followed the path through a herd of cows. The ones grazing lifted their heads slowly, chewing their cud. The ones lying in the grass remained motionless, as solid as toy cows set out on a toy farm. A covey of partridges got up under his feet, making him jump and cry out. They whirred away over the field, their blunt forms travelling as direct as a barrage of shells. Billy snatched a stone up and threw it after them, but they were already out of sight over the hedges. The stone flushed a blackbird, and it chattered away along the hedge bottom, disappearing back into the foliage further along.

He reached the stile which led into the woods, climbed on to it and looked back. Fields and fences and hedgerows. The sun was in the sky, and the only sound was the continuous relay of bird song.

As soon as he entered the wood, Billy left the path and mounted a bank into the undergrowth. He pushed the branches back, away from his eyes, keeping hold until the last moment, then releasing them to thrash back into the foliage behind. He cut a branch off an elm sapling, trimmed it to walking stick length, then used it to fence his way through, slashing and fracturing any limbs in his path.

The undergrowth thinned out, giving way to grassy clearings between the trees. Overhead their branches webbed into a green canopy, and in places shafts of sunlight angled through, dappling the grey-green trunks, and bringing up the colour of the grass and the foliage. Light and shade, a continuous play of light and shade with every rustle of the leaves. Here the bird songs were less frequent, yet more distinct. Hidden somewhere amongst the branches a chaffinch gave out its long undulating notes, concluding each sequence with a flourish. A wood pigeon managed a few series of throaty coo-ings, ending each series with an abrupt 'cu', as though its chest was too sore to carry on. The silence between these calls emphasized the noise of Billy's progress, and birds retreated prematurely before the swishing and snapping : a robin, tic-tic-tic, a pair of wrens, their loud churrs out of all proportion to their mouse-like size, and a jay, its white rump flashing across the bars of the trees.

Billy zig-zagged slowly between the trees, searching any growth round the base of their trunks, then stepping back and looking up into their branches. He high-stepped his way through a bramble patch, trampling the tentacles underfoot as though tramping through deep snow. Below him four beaks opened at the noise, and he crouched down over a thrush's nest. The four young were almost fully fledged, and they fitted the nest as snugly as a completed jig-saw. Billy stroked their backs gently with one finger, then stood up and re-arranged the brambles over the nest before passing on.

He reached a riding and stopped for a minute, resting his back against the trunk of a beech tree. A breeze murmured continually in the tree tops, and it was cool under the foliage of the beech, where the sun didn't penetrate. A broad green stripe scored the grey bark of the tree and when Billy scraped his thumb up it, a skimming of moss came away, as cool and moist as yeast. He crossed the riding and slowly approached a scots pine, looking up all the time at the dark bunch of a nest built high amongst its top whiskers. He stopped beneath it and put his hands in his pockets while he studied the trunk. It was as straight and thick as a telegraph pole. The first fifteen feet were bare, then began a rotten stepladder of stubs and dead branches, leading up to the sparse greenery at the top. He felt round the bark, probing it with his fingers. It was crusty and rough with splits in the stippling. Billy peeled a strip off and squinted up the trunk as though taking aim. He shook his head and walked away, stopped, and started to take his jacket off as he walked back. He spat on his palms, rubbed them together, then, hugging the trunk, began to shin up it. He climbed in segments like a caterpillar, his arms hugging and pulling, his legs gripping and pushing. Up, slowly upwards, fingers scrabbling, pumps rasping. He reached the first dead branch and rested with one foot pressed into the junction of the branch and the trunk. Sweat was dripping from his chin. He looked down, looked up and began to climb again, testing each projection with his hand, and only using it to obtain the slightest leverage. Up, slowly upwards. The trunk began to sway a little and the branches at the top were swaying as though a stiff wind was blowing. He paused directly under the nest and looked round. He was now above many of the trees and the rooves of their foliage stretched round him in green hillocks.

A crow flew in from over the fields, flapping low over the tree tops. Billy froze to the trunk, waiting for it. Then he whistled. The crow planed off and dived into the hillocks like a rabbit diving into its burrow. Billy grinned and felt carefully over the stick wall of the nest. The bowl was stuffed with old leaves and twigs.

'Shit.'

He pulled a handful out and they crackled like crisps as he crushed them and tossed them away.

Ten feet from the ground he pushed himself clear of the trunk and dropped, landing and rolling parachute style. He stood up and looked up at the nest. He was breathing hard and his face was flushed, and when he inspected his palms, the rawness showed through the dirt like the dull red of a cooling poker glowing through the soot.

The wood ended at a hawthorn hedge lining one side of a cart track. Across the track and beyond an orchard stood the Monastery Farm, and at the side of it, the ruins and one remaining wall of the monastery. Billy walked along the hedge bottom, searching for a way through. He found a hole, and as he crawled through a kestrel flew out of the monastery wall and veered away across the fields behind the farm. Billy knelt and watched it. In two blinks it was a speck in the distance; then it wheeled and began to return. Billy hadn't moved a muscle before it was slipping back across the face of the wall towards the cart track.

Half-way across the orchard it started to glide upwards in a shallow curve and alighted neatly on a telegraph pole at the side of the cart track. It looked round, roused its feathers, then crossed its wings over its back and settled. Billy waited for it to turn away, then, watching it all the time, he carefully stretched full length in the hedge bottom. The hawk tensed and stood up straight, and stared past the monastery into the distance. Billy looked in the same direction. The sky was clear. A pair of magpies flew up from the orchard and crossed to the wood, their quick wing-beats seeming to just keep them airborne. They took stance in a tree close by and started to chatter, each sequence of chatterings sounding like one turn of a football rattle. The hawk ignored them and continued the stare into the distance. The sky was still clear. Then a speck appeared on the horizon. It held like a star, then fell and faded. Died. To reappear a moment later further along the skyline. Fading and re-forming, sometimes no more than a point in the texture of the sky. Billy squeezed his eyes and rubbed them. On the telegraph pole the hawk was sleek and still. The dot magnified slowly into its mate, circling and scanning the fields round the farm.

It braked and lay on the air looking down, primaries quivering to catch the currents, tail fanned, tilted towards the earth. Then, angling its wings, it slipped sideways a few yards, fluttered, and started to hover again. Persistently this time, hovering then dropping vertically in short bursts, until it closed its wings and stooped, a breath-taking stoop, down behind a wall. To rise again with its prey secure in its talons and head swiftly back across the fields. The falcon, alert on the pole, screamed and took off to meet it. They both screamed continuously as the distance closed between them, reaching a climax as they met and transferred the prey. The male disappeared over the wood. The falcon swooped high into a hole in the monastery wall. Billy noted the place carefully. A few seconds later the falcon reappeared and planed away over the fields, returning in a wide circle back to the telegraph pole.

Billy settled. Before him the monastery ruins were thronged with sparrows and starlings. Swallows swooped witta-witta-wit around the ruins and the farm, and a pair of them chased

28

amongst the trees of the orchard, the leader flying and dodging so rapidly that it seemed impossible for the pursuer to keep in such close contact.

The wall cast its shadow back over the farmhouse, and from the yard behind the house, a dog barked, two men called to each other and a child laughed out.

Billy selected a stem of grass and carefully drew it up from beneath the leaves. The green faded to white near the bottom of the stem and Billy placed this pale end between his teeth and began to nibble and suck at it. The hawk turned its head and stared up the cart track, then silently lobbed off the telegraph pole and flew away in the opposite direction.

A man appeared round the curve of the cart track. Billy lay still. As he approached, the man took a run at a pebble and side-footed it stylishly along the track. The pebbled bounced across the crusty ridges and disappeared into the hedge bottom. The man smiled, began to whistle and passed by.

Billy rested his head in the crook of his arm and closed his eyes. When he awoke the hawk was back on the pole and the sun was directly above the farm. He yawned and stretched hard, pointing his toes and bracing his hands against the base of a tree. The hawk glanced round and was away as soon as he popped his head through the hole in the hedge. He watched it go, then crossed the track and climbed over the wall into the orchard. He had almost reached the ruins when a little girl playing at the front of the farm-house saw him. She ran round into the yard and returned with her father.

'Hey! What you doing?'

Billy stopped and glanced back towards the wood.

'Nowt.'

'Well bugger off then! Don't you know this is private property?'

'Can I get up to that kestrel's nest?'

'What kestrel's nest?'

Billy pointed at the monastery wall.

'Up that wall.'

'There's no nest up there, so off you go.'

'There is. I've seen it fly in.'

The farmer started to walk across to the ruins. The little girl ran to keep up with him, and Billy backed off, keeping the same distance between them all the time.

'An' what you goin' to do when you get up to it, take all t'eggs?'

'There's no eggs in, they're young 'uns.'

'Well, there's nowt to get up for then, is there?'

'I just wanted to look, that's all.'

'Yes, an' you'd be looking from six feet under if you tried to climb up there.'

'Can I have a look from t'bottom, then?'

The farmer stood under the wall and looked across at him.

'Go on, mister, I've never found a hawk's nest before.'

'Come on, then.'

Billy grinned and sprinted up the edge of the orchard. As soon as he reached the farmer he pointed up at the wall, his finger steady on one spot.

'That's where it is, look, in that hole at t'side o' that window.'

The farmer glanced down on him and smiled.

'I know it is. It's nested here for donkey's years now.'

'Just think, an' I never knew.'

'There's not many does.'

'Have you ever been up to it?'

'No, I've never fancied goin' that high on an extender.'

'I've been watching 'em from across in t'wood. You ought to have seen 'em. One of 'em was sat on that telegraph pole for ages.'

He spun round and pointed to it.

'I was right underneath it, then I saw its mate, it came from miles away and started to hover, just over there.'

Billy started to hover, arms out, fluttering his hands.

'Then it dived down behind that wall and came up wi' summat in its claws. You ought to have seen it, mister, it wa' smashin'.'

The farmer laughed and ruffled the hair of the little girl who was standing just behind him, holding on to his trouser leg.

'We see it every day, don't we, love?'

'It allus sits on that pole, don't it, dad?'

'I wish I could see it every day.'

Billy studied the face of the wall, and his prolonged silence made the farmer and the little girl look up with him. The surface rose in a variegated complex of pitted granite and scooped sandstone. Whole sections had tumbled and the gaps had been patched with bricks, which in turn had eroded and tumbled. In the holes and in the chinks between the stones where the plaster had crumbled, moss and grass grew and birds had stuffed their nests.

'They've been goin' to pull it down for years.'

'What for?'

'It's dangerous. I won't let her play anywhere near it.'

He felt behind his leg. Feeling nothing, he looked round. The little girl was jumping from stone to stone in the ruins.

'Has anybody ever been up?'

'Not that I know of.'

'I bet I could get up.'

'You're not goin' to have chance though.'

'If I lived here, I'd get a young 'un and train it.'

'Would you?'

His tone of inquiry made Billy look up at him.

'You can train 'em.'

'An' how would you go about it?'

Billy held the farmer's gaze, then looked away, nibbling his bottom lip. He concentrated on his pumps for a minute, then looked up quickly.

'Do you know?'

'No, an' there's not many that does.'

'Where could you find out about 'em?'

'That's why I won't let anybody near, 'cos if they can't be kept properly it's criminal.'

'Do you know anybody who's kept one?'

'One or two, but they've allus let 'em go 'cos they couldn't do owt wi' 'em. They never seemed to get tame like other birds.'

'Where could you find out then?'

'I don't know. In books, I suppose. I should think there's some books on falconry.'

'Think there'll be any in t'library?'

'There might be in t'City Library. They've books on everything in there.'

'I'm off then now. So long, mister.'

Billy ran across the field, back the way he had come.

'Hey!'

'What?'

'Go through t'gate! You'll be having that wall down, climbing over it!'

Billy changed direction and ran along the side of the wall, at right angles to his previous course.

'Got any books on hawks, missis?'

The girl behind the counter looked up from sorting coloured tickets in a tray.

'Hawks?'

'I want a book on falconry.'

'I'm not sure, you'd better try ornithology.'

'What's that?'

'Under zoology.'

She leaned over the desk and pointed down a corridor of shelves, then stopped and looked Billy over.

'Are you a member?'

'What do you mean, a member?'

'A member of the library.'

Billy pressed a finger into the ink pad on the desk and inspected the purple graining on the tip.

'I don't know owt about that. I just want to lend a book on falconry, that's all.'

'You can't borrow books unless you're a member.'

'I only want one.'

'Have you filled one of these forms in?'

She licked a forefinger and flicked a blue form up on to her thumb. Billy shook his head.

'Well you're not a member then. Do you live in the Borough?'

'What do you mean?'

'The Borough, the City.'

'No, I live out on Valley Estate.'

'Well that's in the Borough, isn't it?'

A man approached and plonked two books on the counter. The girl attended to him immediately. Open stamp, Open stamp. She slotted the cards into his tickets and filed them in a tray. The man pulled his books to the edge of the counter, caught them as they overbalanced, then shouldered his way through the swinging doors.

'Can I get a book now, then?'

'You'll have to take one of these forms home first for your father to sign.'

She handed Billy a form across the counter. He took it and looked down at the dotted lines and blank boxes.

'My dad's away.'

'You'll have to wait until he comes home then.'

'I don't mean away like that. I mean he's left home.'

'O, I see. . . . Well in that case, your mother'll have to sign it.'

'She's at work.'

'She can sign it when she comes home, can't she?'

'I know, but she'll not be home 'til tea time, and it's Sunday tomorrow.'

'There's no rush, is there?'

'I don't want to wait that long. I want a book today.'

'You'll just have to want, won't you?'

'Look, just let me go an' see 'f you've got one, an' if you have I'll sit down at one o' them tables an' read it.'

'You can't, you're not a member.'

'Nobody'll know.'

'It's against the rules.'

'Go on. I'll bring you this paper back on Monday then.'

'N O ! Now go on home and get that form signed.'

She turned round and entered a little glass office.

'I say.'

Billy beckoned her out.

'Now what?'

'Where's there a bookshop?'

'Well, there's Priors up the Arcade. That's the best one.'

'O ye! I know.'

33

He went out into the sunlight. People crowded the pavements and gutters, and on the road the traffic was jammed honking in two straight lines. Billy screwed the form up and dropped it onto a grate. It bounced on the bars, then fell between them. He squeezed between a car and a bus and jogged down the centre line of the road. Car drivers with their arms resting on window ledges looked up at him as he passed. The vehicles at the head of one line began to move. Billy slipped back on to the pavement before the reaction in the chain could reach him.

He looked in at the window display, then walked through the open doorway and crossed to a rack of paperbacks. Walking round the rack, and revolving it in the opposite direction, he examined the room as it flickered by between the books and the wire struts. All four walls were lined with books. Disposed around the room were racks and stands of paperbacks, and in the centre was a table with a till and piles of books on it. There were three assistants, two girls and a man. Several people were browsing, and one young man was buying. The shop was as quiet as the library.

He started in one corner, and, working from the top shelf, down, up, down, moved along the sections, scanning the categories, which were printed on white cards and stuck on the edges of the shelves: CRAFTS ... DICTIONARIES ... DEVOTIONAL ... FICTION ... GARDENING ... HISTORY ... MOTORING ... NATURE—ANIMALS, one shelf, two shelves. BIRDS, birds, birds. *A Falconer's Handbook.* Billy reached up. The book was clamped tight in the middle of the shelf. He pressed the top of the spine and tilted it towards him, catching it as it fell. He opened it and flicked through it back to front, pausing at the pictures and diagrams. A sparrow-hawk stared up from the glossy paper of the dust jacket. Billy glanced round. The man and one of the girls were serving. The other girl was shelving books with her back to him. Everyone else had their heads down. Billy turned his back on them and slipped the book inside his jacket. The man and the girl continued to serve. The other girl continued to shelve. Billy continued round the walls, to the door, and out into the arcade.

34

'What's tha want that for when tha can't read?'

Jud reached over Billy's shoulder and snatched the book out of his hands. Billy jumped up from the kitchen step and ran after him into the living room.

'Giz it back! Come here!'

Jud held him off, tilting his head and trying to read the title at arm's length as the book flapped open and shut.

'Falconry! What's thar know about falconry?'

'Giz it back.'

Jud pushed him back on to the settee, then started to examine the book at leisure.

'*A Falconer's Handbook*. Where's tha got this from?'

'I've lent it.'

'Nicked it, more like. Where's tha got it from?'

'A shop in town.'

'Tha must be crackers.'

'How's tha mean?'

'Nicking books.'

He looked at a picture, then slapped it shut.

'I could understand it if it wa' money, but chuff me, not a book.'

He skimmed it hard across the room. The covers flapped open and when Billy grabbed at it, he bent and scuffled the pages back.

'Look what tha's done now! I'm trying to look after this book.'

He smoothed the bent pages, then shut the covers and squeezed them tight.

'Anybody's think it wa' a treasure tha'd got.'

'It's smashing! I've been reading it all afternoon, I'm nearly half-way through already.'

'An' what better off will tha be when tha's read it?'

'A lot, 'cos I'm goin' to get a young kestrel an' train it.'

'Train it! Tha couldn't train a flea!'

He laughed out, mouth open, head back, more a roar than a laugh.

'Anyroad, where tha goin' to get a kestrel from?'

'I know a nest.'

'Tha doesn't.'

'All right then, I don't.'

'Where?'

'I'm not telling.'

'I said where?'

He rushed over to the settee and jumped astride Billy, pushing his face into the cushions and forcing one arm up his back in a half-nelson.

'I said where?'

'Gi'o'er, Jud, tha breaking my arm!'

'Where then?'

'Monastery Farm.'

Jud let go and cuffed Billy's scalp as he stood up. Billy sat up, rubbing the tears from his cheeks and massaging his arm.

'You fool, tha nearly broke my arm then.'

'I'll have to see about goin' round there wi' t'gun.'

'I'll tell t'farmer on thi if tha does.'

'What's he got to do wi' it?'

'He protects 'em.'

'Protects 'em! Don't talk wet! Hawks are a menace to farmers, they eat all their poultry an' everything.'

'I know, they dive down on their cows an' carry 'em away an' all.'

'Funny bugger.'

'We' tha talks daft! How big's tha think they are? Kestrels only eat mice an' insects an' little birds sometimes.'

'Tha think tha knows summat about it, don't tha?'

'I know more about it than thee, anyroad.'

'Tha ought to, tha near lives round them bleedin' woods. It's a wonder tha don't turn into a wild man.'

He stuffed his tongue under his bottom lip, grunting and scratching his armpits. Then he straightened up, grinning.

'Billy Casper! Wild man of the woods! I ought to have thi in a cage. I'd make a bloody fortune.'

Billy scrambled up off the settee and raised his arms laterally, beating the air with short powerful strokes.

'Tha should have seen 'em today though, lad, they go like lightning!'

He held his arms still and angled them by flexing his trunk laterally.

'I laid watchin' 'em for hours. They're t'best things I've ever seen.'

Jud watched him through the mirror, chin up, throat taut as he knotted his tie.

'I'm hopin' I'll be laid watchin' a bird tonight. But she'll not have feathers on; not all over anyway.'

He grinned at himself and folded his collar down, covering the back of the tie.

'Tha ought to have seen 'em though Jud.'

'A few pints first.'

'An' tha ought to have seen one of them dive down.'

'Then straight across to t'Lyceum.'

'It dived straight down behind this wall. Whoosh!'

Billy clawed his fingers, and dived straight down on to the settee. Mrs Casper came in from the hall, looking down at herself and smoothing wrinkles out of her sweater. Every time she brushed her palms down the front, her breasts flubbered underneath.

'You're a couple o' noisy buggers, you two. I bet they can hear you at t'other side o' t'estate. What you been making him roar for, Jud?'

'I never touched him.'

'Not much! He nearly broke my arm, that's all.'

'I'll break thi neck next time.'

'O shut it, both of you.'

'We' he's nowt but a big baby.'

'An' thar nowt but a big bully.'

'I said S H U T I T.'

She stood between them, looking from one to the other; then moved across to the fireplace and looked into the mirror.

'Have you had any tea yet, Billy?'

'No.'

'Well get some then, you know where t'pantry is.'

'He's too busy reading to bother about eating.'

'How did your horses get on today, Jud?'

'Not bad, I'd a double up.'

'How much?'

'Enough.'

'You'll be treating us all tonight, then?'

'There's somebody treats you every night.'

'It'd be nice. Shift, Billy.'

She pulled Billy to the front of the settee and dragged a cushion out from behind him. Underneath it was a pair of stockings as flat as flowers in a book. She held them up to the window, inspecting them in lengths, then lifted a foot on to the settee and began to roll one on.

'Where you going tonight then, Jud, anywhere special?'

'Usual I suppose.'

'And don't be coming home blind drunk again.'

'Why, are you entertaining?'

'Don't be so cheeky.'

'Anyway, you want to talk about coming home drunk.'

'I never come home drunk.'

'Not much you don't.'

'Well at least I'm not sick all over t'house every Saturday night.'

'Not this house perhaps.'

'And what's that suppose to mean?'

'Well you don't come here every Saturday night, do you?'

'Seen my shoes, Billy, love?'

She looked round, under the chairs and table, then knelt down and felt under the settee. Jud slipped his suit jacket on and flexed his shoulders, smiling at himself in profile through the mirror.

'Some bird's goin' to be lucky tonight.'

He fluffed the bob at the front of his hair and walked out whistling.

Mrs Casper turned her shoes over in her hands, licking her fingers and trying to erase the scuff marks on the heels, then she breathed all over them and rubbed them up on the edge of the tablecloth.

'These could have done with a polish. Still, ne'er mind, it'll soon be dark.'

She stepped into them and looked round at the backs of her legs.

'There's no ladders in these stockings, is there, Billy?'

Billy looked at her legs and shook his head.

'I can't see any.'

'That's summat anyway. What you going to do wi' yourself tonight, love.'

'Read my book.'

'That's nice. What's it about.'

'Falconry. I'm goin' to get a young kestrel an' train it.'

'A kestrel, what's that?'

'A kestrel hawk, what do you think it is?'

'I say, what time is it?'

'I've cleaned t'bottom shed out ready, an' I've built a little nesting box out of an orange box 'til . . .'

'Ten to eight! Ee, I'm goin' to be late as usual.'

She ran into the hall and started to search through a heap of clothes draped over the bannister, peeling them off and throwing them down until she came to her coat.

'Here, there's two bob for you. Go and buy yourself some pop an' some crisps or summat.'

She slid the florin on to the mantelpiece and smiled at herself through the mirror.

'And don't be still up when I come in.'

She hurried through the kitchen and banged the door, leaving the house quiet behind her. Billy opened his book, pointed to his place and began to lip the words as his finger crept under the lines.

*

At the first sound of footsteps on the stairs he slipped the book under the pillow and ran across to the light switch. The footsteps were heavy, their progress punctuated by halts that suggested each time that the climb had been abandoned.

But eventually they reached the top, the light clicked on and Jud swayed into the bedroom, droning. He stopped at the foot of the bed, re-adjusting his feet continually, as though the floor was in motion.

'Billy. Are tha shleep, Billy?'

Billy lay still, his face hidden in the sheet. Jud drifted away and started to fumble at the top button of his shirt, grimacing and trying to squint down at it. His respiration appeared to be out of all proportion to the amount of energy required for this simple task, resembling more the exertions of a cross-country runner. He managed the top two buttons then tugged the shirt over his head, pulling it inside out as he wrenched his hands through the buttoned cuffs. He dropped his trousers and raised one foot. As soon as he leaned forward and looked down, he overbalanced, and had to break into a hop to remain upright. The wall stopped him. He grinned at a rose on the wallpaper, then turned round, covering the rose with his head.

'Whoa you bugger, whoa.'

He rested on the wall, grinning down at the trousers bunched round his ankles.

'Billy! Wake up, Billy!'

He set off across the room like a man in fetters.

'Billy, wake up!'

He stopped at the side of the bed and tried to haul the sheet in.

Billy turned over and tried to hang on to it.

'Gi'o'er, Jud, I'm asleep.'

'Hel' me ge' undresh, Billy. Am pish. Am too pish to take my trouser off.'

He flopped down on to the bed giggling. Billy wriggled out from underneath him and got out of bed. Jud curled up on his side and closed his eyes, a blind smile on his face.

'Turn light osh, Billy, an' ge' to bed.'

Billy turned him on to his back and took his shoes off. He worked his trouser bottoms over his heels, then pulled them over his feet and off.

'I'm fed up o' this bloody game. It's every Saturday night alike!'

Jud was asleep, snoring, mouth open.

'Just like a pig snoring. . . . A drunken pig. . . . Jud the drunken pig.'

He snapped Jud's mouth shut and held his lips between his

finger and thumb. Jud began to grumble in his throat, then he tossed his head free and his eyelids fluttered.

'W'a's up? W'a's up?'

'Get back to sleep ... you pig ... hog ... sow ... you drunken bastard ... Tha don't like being called a bastard, does tha, you bastard? You PIG,' – clawing at Jud with his right hand 'HOG,' – left hand. 'SOW,' – right again. 'DRUNKEN BASTARD,' – one strike per syllable.

'Pig Hog Sow Drun-ken Bas-tard.
Pig Hog Sow Drun-ken Bas-tard.'

Slowly, padding round the bed, clawing, chanting with every step.

Bas-tard, Bas-tard, Drun-ken PIG.
Bas-tard, Bas-tard, Drun-ken PIG.

Faster louder round the bed.

Pig Hog Sow, Drunken Bastard.
Pig Hog Sow, Drunken Bastard.
Bastard Bastard Drunken PIG.

Bastard Bastard Drunken SMACK – Already committed to its strike, Billy's claw had involuntarily hardened to a fist, and thumped Jud, smack on his ear as he turned over on to his side.

For a second, a still, catching Billy poised over the bed, fist still clenched above the offended ear. Then the monster began to rumble. Billy snatched his clothes off the chair, flicked off the light as he ran past, and ran downstairs. His fingers almost seized up as they fumbled at the lock on the kitchen door, their ineptitude making him glance round and squeal softly in fear and excitement. With the door opened, he relaxed and paused on the step to listen. Silence. Continuing silence. So he went back inside and fetched his jacket and pumps, and dressed at leisure in the doorway, by the light of the moon.

The moon was almost complete, its outline well defined, except for the blur on the waxing curve. The sky was cloudless, the air still warm, but when he reached the fields it cooled slightly, taking on a fresher, sharper quality. The moon made it light in the fields, and lent the grass a silver sheen, and the piebald hides of the cows were clearly visible in this silvery light. The wood was a narrow black band beyond the fields, growing taller and taller as Billy approached, until it formed a curtain stretched out before him, and the top of the curtain appeared to touch the stars directly above.

He climbed on to the stile and looked into the trees. It was dark on both sides of the path, but above the path the foliage was thinner, and the light from the moon penetrated and lit the way. Billy stepped down off the stile and entered the wood. The trunks and branches lining the path formed pillars and lintels, terraced doorways leading into dark interiors. He hurried by them, glancing in, right and left. A scuffle to his left. He side-stepped to the right and began to run, the pad of his feet and the rasp of his breath filtering far into the trees. WO-HU-WO-HOOOO. WO-HU-WO-HOOOO. He stopped and listened, trying to control his breathing. WO-HU-WO-HOOO. Somewhere ahead; the long falter radiating back through the trees. Billy linked his fingers, placed his thumbs together and blew into the split between them. The only sound he produced was that of rushing air. He licked his lips and tried again, producing a wheeze, which he swiftly worked up into a single hoot and developed into a strident imitation of the tawny owl's call. He listened. There was no response, so he repeated it, this time working for the softer, more wavering sound, by stuttering his breath into the sound chamber. And out it came, as clear and as clean as a blowing of bubbles. His call was immediately answered. Billy grinned and answered back. He started to walk again, and maintained contact with the owl for the rest of the distance through the wood.

The farmhouse was in darkness. Billy carefully climbed over the wall into the orchard and ran crouching across to the ruins. He stood back from the wall and looked up at it. The moon illuminated the face of the wall, picking out the jut of individual stones, and shading in the cracks and hollows between them. Billy selected his route, found a foothold, a handhold, and began to climb. Very slowly and very carefully, testing each hold thoroughly before trusting it with his weight. His fingers finding the spaces, then tugging at the surrounding stones as though testing loose teeth. If any stones moved he felt again, remaining still until he was satisfied. Slowly. Hand. Foot. Hand. Foot. Never stretching, never jerking. Always compact, always balanced. Sometimes crabbing to by-pass gaps in the stonework, sometimes back-tracking several moves to explore a new line; but steadily meandering upwards, making for the highest window.

As he climbed, his feet and hands dislodged a trickle of plaster and stone dust, and birds brushed his knuckles as they flashed out of their nest holes. Occasionally he dislodged a small stone or a lump of plaster, and when he felt this happen he paused during the time of its fall, and for a time after it had landed.

But there were no alarms, and he reached the window and hooked his left arm over the stone sill. He slapped the stone and sh sh'd at the hole at the other end of the sill. Nothing happened so he climbed astride and hutched across to the next hole. He peered in, but there was nothing to see, so he stretched belly flop along the sill and felt into the hole, wriggling further along as his arm went further in. He felt around, then withdrew his hand grasping a struggling eyas kestrel. He sat up, caged the bird in his hands, then placed it carefully into the big pocket inside his jacket. Five times he felt into the hole and each time fetched out a young hawk. Some were slightly larger than others, some more fully feathered, with less down on their backs and heads, but each one came out gasping, beaks open, legs pedalling the air.

When he had emptied the nest he reversed the procedure, dipping into his pocket for an eyas and holding it in one hand while he compared it with another. By a process of elimination, he placed them back into the nest until he was left with only one; the one with most feathers and only a little down on its head. He lowered it back into the pocket, then held his hand up to catch the light of the moon. Both back and palm were bleeding and scratched, as though he had been nesting in a hawthorn hedge.

When he reached the bottom of the wall he opened his jacket and clucked down into the pocket. The weight at the bottom stirred. He placed one hand underneath it for support, and set off back across the orchard. Once over the wall, he started to whistle, and he whistled and hummed to himself all the way home...

... Billy had been standing so still that the hawk had lost interest in him, and flew from the shelf to the perch at the back of the shed. He put his face close to the bars, had a last look at her, then turned away and walked up the path and across the estate to school.

Anderson?	Sir!	/
Armitage?	Yes Sir!	/
Bridges?	Away Sir.	o
Casper?	Yes Sir!	/
Ellis?	Here Sir!	/
Fisher?	German Bight.	/

Mr Crossley dug the Biro point in. Too late, the black stroke skidded diagonally down the square. He lifted his face slowly to the class. All the boys were looking at Billy.

'What was that?'

'It was Casper, Sir.'

'Did you say something, Casper?'

'Yes Sir, I didn't ...'

'Stand up!'

Billy stood up, red. The boys looked up at him, grinning, lolling back on their chairs in anticipation.

'Now then, Casper, what did you say?'

'German Bight, Sir.'

The rest of the class laughed out, some screwing their fore-fingers into their temples and twitching their heads at Billy.

'He's crackers, Sir!'

'He can't help it.'

'SILENCE.'

There was silence.

'Is this your feeble idea of a joke, Casper?'

'No, Sir.'

'Well what was the idea then?'

'I don't know, Sir. It wa' when you said Fisher. It just came out, Fisher – German Bight. It's the shipping forecast, Sir; German Bight comes after Fisher; Fisher, German Bight, Cromarty. I know 'em all, I listen to it every night, I like to hear the names.'

'And so you thought you'd enlighten me and the class with your idiotic information?'

'No, Sir.'

'Blurting out and making a mess of my register.'

'It just came out, Sir.'

'And so did you, Casper. Just came out from under a stone.'

The class roared out again, tossing their heads back and scraping their chairs, banging their desk lids and thumping the backs and arms of any boy in range; using the joke as a mere excuse to cause havoc.

'Quiet! I said QUIET.'

His gaze raked the class, killing the sound in each face. The bell rang. Crossley fixed Billy with his eyes all the time it was ringing, and for a while after it had stopped.

'Any more pearls of wisdom to volunteer, Casper?'

'No, Sir.'

'Well SIT DOWN THEN.'

Billy sat down, sliding down his seat until his hair scuffed the top rung of the chair back. Crossley moved his Biro back to the register, cocking it vertical like a fishing float. Outside the room the corridor was crowded with children moving to assembly.

'Anyone else absent besides Bridges and Fisher?'

Pause for inspection.

'No, Sir.'

'Right, off you go then. One row at a time.'

The boys lolloped up into the aisles, merging at the door into a tributary of the mainstream in the corridor.

'Hey up, Casper, what's tha mean, Germans bite?'

'O shut thi mouth.'

Crossley marked off the remainder of the 'present' strokes, then changed his black Biro for red, and, very carefully, bending low over the register, tried to bend Fisher's stroke into an o, lapping and lapping the tiny square until he had gouged a mis-coloured egg, the focal point of the whole grid.

'Hymn number one-seven-five, "New every morning is the love".'

The navy blue covers of the hymn books, inconspicuous against the dark shades of the boys' clothing, bloomed white across the hall as they were opened and the pages flicked through. The scuff and tick of the turning pages was slowly drowned under a rising chorus of coughing and hawking; until Mr Gryce, furious behind the lectern, scooped up his stick and began to smack it vertically down the face.

'STOP THAT INFERNAL COUGHING.'

The sight and swishsmack of the stick stopped the throat noises and the boys and the teachers, posted at regular intervals at the ends of the rows; all looked up at the platform. Gryce was straining over the top of the lectern like a bulldog up on its hind legs.

'It's every morning alike! As soon as the hymn is announced you're off revving up! Hm-hmm! Hm-hmm! It's more like a race track in here than an assembly hall!' – hall – ringing across the hall, striking the windows and lingering there like the vibrations of a tuning fork.

No one muffed. Not a foot scraped. Not a page stirred. The teachers looked seriously into the ranks of boys. The boys stood looking up at Gryce, each one convinced that Gryce was looking at him.

The silence thickened; the boys began to swallow their Adam's apples, their eyes skittering about in still heads. The teachers began to glance at each other and glance sideways up at the platform.

Then a boy coughed.

'Who did that?'

Everybody looking round.

'I said WHO DID THAT?'

The teachers moved in closer, alert like a riot squad.

'Mr Crossley! Somewhere near you! Didn't you see the boy?'

Crossley flushed, and rushed amongst them, thrusting them aside in panic.

'There, Crossley! That's where it came from! Around there!'

Crossley grabbed a boy by the arm and began to yank him into the open.

'It wasn't me, Sir!'

'Of course it was you.'

'It wasn't, Sir, honest!'

'Don't argue lad, I saw you.'

Gryce thrust his jaw over the front of the lectern, the air whistling down his nostrils.

'MACDOWALL! I might have known it! Get to my room, lad!'

Crossley escorted MacDowall from the hall. Gryce waited for the doors to stop swinging, then replaced his stick and addressed the school.

'Right. We'll try again. Hymn one hundred and seventy-five.'

The pianist struck the chord. Moderately slow it said in the book, but this direction was ignored by the school, and the tempo they produced was dead slow, the words delivered in a grinding monotone.

> 'New ev-ery morn-ing is the love
> Our waken-ing and up-ris-ing prove;
> Through sleep and dark-ness safe-ly brought,
> Re-stored to life, and power, and thought.'

'STOP.'

The pianist stopped playing. The boys stopped singing.

'And what's that noise supposed to represent? I've heard sweeter sounds in a slaughter house! This is supposed to be a hymn of joy, not a dirge! So get your heads up, and your books up, and open your mouths, and SING.'

There was a mass bracing of backs and showing of faces as Gryce stepped round the lectern to the edge of the platform and leaned out over the well of the hall.

'Or I'll make you sing like you've never sung before.'

The words came out in a whisper, but they were as audible to the older boys at the back of the hall as to the small boys staring up under his chin.

'Verse two – New mercies each returning day.'

Gryce retreated, and the remaining four verses were completed without interruption, verse two with increased volume, deteriorating through three and four, to the concluding verse, which was delivered in the original monotone.

Before all the hymn books had been closed, and with the last notes still in the air, a boy came forward from the drapes at the back of the platform, and while still in motion began to read from the Bible held close to his chest.

'Thismorning'sreadingistakenfromMattheweighteenverses ...'

'Louder, boy. And stop mumbling into your beard.'

'Never despise one of these little ones I tell you they have their guardian angels in heaven who look continually on the face of my heavenly Father. What do you think suppose a man has a hundred sheep if one of them strays does he not leave the other ninety-nine on the hillside and go in search of the one that strayed. And if he should find it I tell you this he is more delighted over that sheep than over the ninety-nine that never strayed. In the same way it is your heavenly Father's will that one of these little ones should be lost here ends this morning's reading.'

He closed the Bible and backed away, his relief pathetic to see.

'We will now sing the Lord's Prayer. Eyes closed. Heads bowed.'

Billy closed his eyes and yawned down his nostrils into his chest.

'Our Fa-ther which art in heaven,

Hallowed be Thy name. He unlocked the shed door, slipped inside and closed it quietly behind him. The hawk was perched on a branch which had been wedged between the walls towards the back of the shed. The only other furniture in the shed were two shelves, one fixed behind the bars of the door, the other high up on the wall. The walls and ceiling were whitewashed, and the floor had been sprinkled with a thick layer of dry sand, sprinkled thicker beneath the perch and the shelves. The shelf on the door was marked with two dried mutes, both thick and

white, with a central deposit of faeces as crozzled and black as
the burnt ends of matches.

Billy approached the hawk slowly, regarding it obliquely,
clucking and chanting softly, 'Kes Kes Kes.' The hawk bobbed
her head and shifted along the perch. Billy held out his gauntlet
and offered her a scrap of beef. She reached forward and
grasped it with her beak, and tried to pull it from his glove.
Billy gripped the beef tightly between forefinger and thumb; and
in order to obtain more leverage, the hawk stepped on to his
fist. He allowed her to take the beef, then replaced her on the
perch, touching the backs of her legs against the wood so that
she stepped backwards on to it. He dipped into the leather satchel at his hip and offered her a fresh scrap; this time holding it
just out of range of her reaching beak. She bobbed her head and
tippled forward slightly, regained balance, then glanced about,
uncertain, like someone up on the top board for the first time.

'Come on, Kes. Come on then.'

He stood still. The hawk looked at the meat, then jumped on
to the glove and took it. Billy smiled and replaced it with a
tough strip of beef, and as the hawk busied herself with it, he
attached a swivel to the ends of the jesses dangling from her
legs, slipped the jesses between the first and second fingers of
his glove, and felt into his bag for the leash. The hawk looked
up from her feeding. Billy rubbed his finger and thumb to make
the meat move between them, and as the hawk attended to it
again, he threaded the leash through the lower ring of the swivel
and pulled it all the way through until the knot at the other end
snagged on the ring. He completed the security by looping the
leash twice round his glove and tying the end round his little
finger.

He walked to the door and slowly pushed it open. The hawk
looked up, and as he moved out into the full light, her eyes
seemed to expand, her body contract as she flattened her feathers. She bobbed her head, once, twice, then bated, throwing herself sideways off his glove and hanging upside down, thrashing
her wings and screaming. Billy waited for her to stop, then
placed his hand gently under her breast and lifted her back on
to the glove. She bated again; and again, and each time Billy

lifted her carefully back up, until finally she stayed up, beak half open, panting, glaring round.

'What's up then? What's a matter with you, Kes? Anybody'd think you'd never been out before.'

The hawk roused her feathers and bent to her meat, her misdemeanours apparently forgotten.

Billy walked her round the garden, speaking quietly to her all the time. Then he turned up the path at the side of the house and approached the front gate, watching the hawk for her reactions. A car approached. The hawk tensed, watched it pass, then resumed her meal as it sped away up the avenue. On the opposite pavement a little boy, pedalling a tricycle round in tight circles, looked up and saw them, immediately unwound and drove straight off the pavement, making the tin mudguards clank as the wheels jonked down into the gutter. Billy held the hawk away from him, anticipating a bate, but she scarcely glanced up at the sound, or at the boy as he cycled towards them and hutched his tricycle up on the pavement.

'Oo that's a smasher. What is it?'

'What tha think it is?'

'Is it an owl?'

'It's a kestrel.'

'Where you got it from?'

'Found it.'

'Is it tame?'

'It's trained. I've trained it.'

Billy pointed to himself, and smiled across at the hawk.

'Don't it look fierce?'

'It is.'

'Does it kill things and eat 'em?'

'Course it does. It kills little kids on bikes.'

The boy laughed without smiling.

'It don't.'

'What's tha think that is it's eating now then?'

'It's only a piece of meat.'

'It's a piece o' leg off a kid it caught yesterday. When it catches 'em it sits on their handlebars and rips 'em to pieces. Eyes first.'

50

The boy looked down at the chrome handlebars and began to swing them from side to side, making the front wheel describe a steady arc like a windscreen wiper.

'I'll bet I dare stroke it.'

'Tha'd better not.'

'I'll bet I dare.'

'It'll have thi hand off if tha tries.'

The boy stood up, straddling the tricycle frame, and slowly lifted one hand towards the hawk. She mantled her wings over the meat, then struck out with her scaly yellow legs, screaming, and raking at the hand with her talons. The boy jerked his arm back with such force that its momentum carried his whole body over the tricycle and on to the ground. He scrambled up, as wide-eyed as the hawk, mounted, and pedalled off down the pavement, his legs whirring like bees' wings.

Billy watched him go, then opened the gate and walked up the avenue. He crossed at the top and walked down the other side to the cul-de-sac, round, and back up to his own house. And all the way round people stared, some crossing the avenue for a closer look, others glancing back. And the hawk, alert to every movement, returned their stares until they turned away and passed on.

'Casper! Casper!' Billy opened his eyes. The rest of the school were sitting on the floor, giggling up at him. Billy glanced about, then blushed and dropped down as quick as a house of cards.

'Up, Casper! Up on your feet, lad!'

There was a moment's pause, then Billy rose into view again, his reappearance produced a buzz of excitement.

'SILENCE — unless some more of you want to stand up with him.'

Gryce let Billy stand there in the silence, head bowed, face burning on his chest.

'And get your head up lad! Or you'll be falling asleep again!'

Billy lifted his face. Beads of sweat were poised on his forehead and the sides of his nose.

'You were asleep weren't you? . . . Well? Speak up, lad!'

'I don't know, Sir.'

'Well I know. You were fast asleep on your feet. Weren't you?'

'Yes, Sir.'

'Fast asleep during the Lord's Prayer! I'll thrash you, you irreverent scoundrel!'

He demonstrated the act twice down the side of the lectern.

'Were you tired, lad?'

'I don't know, Sir.'

'Don't know? You wouldn't be tired if you'd get to bed at night instead of roaming the streets at all hours up to mischief!'

'No, Sir.'

'Or sitting up 'til dawn watching some tripe on television! Report to my room straight after assembly. You will be tired when I've finished with you, lad!'

Billy sat down, and Gryce pulled a thin wad of papers from between the pages of the Bible and placed them on top of it.

'Now here are the announcements: – there will be a meeting of the Intermediate Football Team in the gym at break this morning.'

He slid the top sheet down a step, on to the face of the lectern.

'A reminder that the Youth Employment Officer will be in this afternoon to see the Easter leavers. They will be sent for from their respective classes, and should report to the medical room, where the interviews will take place. Your parents SHOULD have been told by this time, but if any boy HAS forgotten, and thinks that his parents may wish to attend his interview, then he can consult the list on the main notice board for approximate times.'

Securing the papers underneath with one hand, he pushed the notice away from him with the other. It caught the edge of the first sheet and shunted it off the lectern. Gryce grabbed at it, but the paper swooped away in a shallow glide, looped the loop, and slid into a perfect landing face up on the platform. Gryce looked across at it, and at the rows of upturned faces, then beckoned the reader from the back of the platform to come forward and pick it up.

'I would also like to see the three members of the smokers' union whom I didn't have time to deal with yesterday. They can pay their dues at my room straight after assembly. Right. Dismiss.'

The three smokers, MacDowall and Billy stood in a loose circle in the foyer outside Gryce's room.

'It wasn't me that coughed tha knows. I'm going to tell him so an' all.'

'It makes no difference whether tha tells him or not, he don't listen.'

'I'm bringing my father up if he giz me t'stick, anyroad.'

'What tha allus bringin' thi father up for? He never does owt when he comes. They say t'last time he came up, Gryce gave him t'stick an' all.'

The three smokers fell away and leaned back on the half-tiled wall to observe.

'At least I've got a father to bring up, that's more than thar can say, Casper.'

'Shut thi gob, MacDowall!'

'Why, what thar goin' to do about it, Casper?'

They closed up; chest to chest, eye to eye, fists ready at the hips.

'Tha'd be surprised.'

'Right then, I'll see thi at break.'

'Anytime tha wants.'

'Right then.'

'Right.'

They stepped apart at footsteps approaching down the corridor. A boy came round the corner and knocked on Gryce's door.

'He's not in.'

The smoker at the front of the queue jerked his head towards the back.

'If tha's come for t'stick tha'd better get to t'back o' t'queue. he's not come back from assembly yet.'

'I've not come for the stick. Crossley's sent me with a message.'

Billy took his place in the line against the wall.

'It's his favourite trick, this. He likes to keep you waiting, he thinks it makes it worse.'

The second smoker spat between his teeth and spread it with the sole of one shoe, making the red vinyl tile shiny.

'It don't bother me if he keeps us standing here 'til four. I'd sooner have t'stick anyday than do lessons.'

He began to feel in his pockets, collecting together in one palm a bunch of tab ends and a lighter without a cap. He offered them to the messenger.

'Here, tha'd better save us these 'til after. Cos if he searches us he'll only take 'em off us an' gi' us another two strokes.'

The messenger looked down at the hand without taking its contents. The other two smokers were busy in their own pockets.

'I'm not having 'em, you're not getting me into trouble as well.'

'Who's getting thi into trouble? Tha can gi' us 'em straight back after.'

The messenger shook his head.

'I don't want 'em.'

'Does tha want some fist instead?'

The smokers surrounded him, all three holding out their smoking equipment. The messenger took it. Billy, looking across the foyer and through the wired glass doors into the hall, stood up off the wall.

'Hey up, he's here; Gryce pudding.'

They formed up as neatly as a hand of cards being knocked together. Gryce strode past them and entered his room as though they weren't there. But he left the door open, and a moment later issued his usual invitation to enter:

'Come in, you reprobates!'

He was standing with his back to the electric fire, his stick tucked under his buttocks like a trapeze bar.

The boys lined up in front of the window and faced him across the carpet. Gryce surveyed them in turn, shaking his head at each face as though he was being forced to choose from a range of shoddy goods.

54

'The same old faces. Why is it always the same old faces?'

The messenger stepped forward and raised one hand.

'Please, Sir.'

'Don't interrupt, boy, when I'm speaking.'

He stepped back and filled the gap in the line.

'I'm sick of you boys, you'll be the death of me. Not a day goes by without me having to deal with a line of boys. I can't remember a day, not one day, in all the years I've been in this school, and how long's that? ... ten years, and the school's no better now than it was on the day that it opened. I can't understand it. I can't understand it at all.'

The boys couldn't understand it either, and they dropped their eyes as he searched for an answer in their faces. Failing to find one there, he stared past them out of the window.

The lawn stretching down to the front railings was studded with worm casts, and badly in need of its Spring growth. The border separating the lawn from the drive was turned earth, and in the centre of the lawn stood a silver birch tree in a little round bed. Its trunk cut a segment out of a house across the road, and out of the merging grey and black of the sky above it, and although the branches were still bare, the white of the trunk against the dull green, and red and greys, hinted of Spring, and provided the only clean feature of the whole picture.

'I've taught in this city for over thirty-five years now; many of your parents were pupils under me in the old city schools before this estate was built; and I'm certain that in all those years I've never encountered a generation as difficult to handle as this one. I thought I understood young people, I should be able to with all my experience, yet there's something happening today that's frightening, that makes me feel that it's all been a waste of time.... Like it's a waste of time standing here talking to you boys, because you won't take a blind bit of notice what I'm saying. I know what you're thinking now, you're thinking, why doesn't he get on with it and let us go, instead of standing there babbling on? That's what you're thinking isn't it? Isn't it, MacDowall?'

'No, Sir.'

'O yes it is. I can see it in your eyes, lad, they're glazed over.

You're not interested. Nobody can tell you anything, can they, MacDowall? You know it all, you young people, you think you're so sophisticated with all your *gear* and your music. But the trouble is, it's only superficial, just a sheen with nothing worthwhile or solid underneath. As far as I can see there's been no advance at all in discipline, decency, manners or morals. And do you know how I know this? Well, I'll tell you. Because I still have to use this every day.'

He brought the stick round from behind his back for the boys to have a look at.

'It's fantastic isn't it, that in this day and age, in this super-scientific, all-things-bright-and-splendiferous age, that the only way of running this school efficiently is by the rule of the cane. But why? There should be no need for it now. You lot have got it on a plate.

'I can understand why we had to use it back in the 'twenties and 'thirties. Those were hard times; they bred hard people, and it needed hard measures to deal with them. But those times bred people with qualities totally lacking in you people today. They bred people with respect for a start. We knew where we stood in those days, and even today a man will often stop me in the street and say "Hello Mr Gryce, remember me?" And we'll pass the time of day and chat, and he'll laugh about the thrashings I gave him.

'But what do I get from you lot? A honk from a greasy youth behind the wheel of some big second-hand car. Or an obscene remark from a gang – after they've passed me.

'They took it then, but not now, not in this day of the common man, when every boy quotes his rights, and shoots off home for his father as soon as I look at him. ... No guts. ... No backbone ... you've nothing to commend you whatsoever. You're just fodder for the mass media!'

He slashed the stick in front of their chests, making the air swish in its wake, then he turned round and leaned straight-armed on the mantelshelf, shaking his head. The boys winked at each other.

'I don't know. I just don't know.'

He turned round slowly. The boys met him with serious ex-

56

pressions, frowning and compressing their lips as though they were trying their hardest to solve his problems.

'So for want of a better solution I continue using the cane, knowing full well that you'll be back time and time again for some more. Knowing that when you smokers leave this room wringing your hands, you'll carry on smoking just the same. Yes, you can smirk, lad. I'll bet your pockets are ladened up at this very moment in readiness for break; aren't they? Aren't they? Well just empty them. Come on, all of you, empty your pockets!'

The three smokers, Billy and MacDowall began to reveal their collected paraphernalia. The messenger watched them in panic, the colour rising in his face like the warming bar of an electric fire. He stepped forward again.

'Please, Sir ...'

'Quiet, lad! And get your pockets emptied!'

The lad's face cooled to the colour of dripping as he began to empty his pockets. Gryce moved along the line, broddling in their palms; turning and inspecting the grubby contents with obvious distaste.

'This can't be true. I don't believe it.'

He placed his stick on his desk.

'Keep your hands out.'

And started down the line again, frisking their clothing quickly and expertly. When he reached the messenger he beamed at him.

'Ah! Ah!'

'Please, Sir ...'

The smokers leaned forward and looked at him, half turning and angling across each other like a prioll of Jacks. They squared their jaws and showed him their teeth. Tears came into the messenger's eyes and he began to snuffle.

'You're a regular cigarette factory aren't you, lad?'

From various pockets Gryce collected two ten-packets, which rattled when he shook them, a handful of tabs, three lighters and a box of matches.

'You deceitful boy. You didn't think you could get away with a weak trick like that, did you?'

He strode over to the basket at the side of his desk and dropped the lot into it.

'Now get that other junk back into your pockets, and get your hands out.'

He picked his stick up from his desk and tested it on the air. The first smoker stepped out and raised his right hand. He proffered it slightly cupped, thumb tucked into the side, the flesh of the palm ruttled up into soft cushions.

Gryce measured the distance with the tip of his stick, settled his feet, then slowly flexed his elbow. When his fist was level with his ear, the hinge flashed open swish down across the boy's palm. The boy blinked and held up his left hand. The stick touched it, curved up and away out of Gryce's peripheral vision, then blurred back into it and snapped down across the fingers.

'Right, now get out.'

White-faced, he turned away from Gryce, and winked at the others as he passed in front of them to the door.

'Next.'

They stepped forward in turn, all adopting the same relaxed hand position as the first boy. Except for the messenger. He presented his hands stiff, fingers splayed, thumbs up. The full force of both strokes caught him thumbs first, cracking across the side of the knuckle bone. The first stroke made him cry. The second made him sick.

*

They all turned their heads when the door opened and Billy walked into the room. Mr Farthing, perched side-saddle on the edge of the desk, stopped talking and waited for him to approach.

'I've been to see Mr Gryce, Sir.'

'Yes, I know. How many this time?'

'Two.'

'Sting?'

'Not bad.'

'Right, sit down then.'

He watched Billy to his place and waited for the class to settle before he continued.

'Right 4C. To continue. Fact.'

He swung one arm and indicated the board behind him. On it was printed:

FACT AND FICTION

'What did we say fact was, Armitage?'

'Something that's happened, Sir.'

'Right. Something that has happened. Something that we know is real. The things that we read about in newspapers, or hear on the news. Events, accidents, meetings; the things that we see with our own eyes, the things all about us; all these are facts. Have you got that? Is that clear?'

Chorus: 'Yes, Sir.'

'Right then. Now if I asked Anderson for some facts about himself, what could he tell us?'

'Sir! Sir!'

'All right! All right! Just put your hands up. There's no need to jump down my throat. Jordan?'

'He's wearing jeans.'

'Good. Mitchell?'

'He's got black hair.'

'Yes. Fisher?'

'He lives down Shallowbank Crescent.'

'Do you, Anderson?'

'Yes, Sir.'

'Right then. Now all these are facts about Anderson, but they're not particularly interesting facts. Perhaps Anderson can tell us something about himself that *is* interesting. A really interesting fact.'

There was a massive 'Woooo!' from the rest of the class. Mr Farthing grinned and rode it; then he raised his hands to control it.

'Quietly now. Quietly.'

The class quietened, still grinning. Anderson stared at his desk, blushing.

'I don't know owt, Sir.'

'Anything at all Anderson, anything that's happened to you, or that you've seen which sticks in your mind.'

'I can't think of owt, Sir.'

'What about when you were little? Everybody remembers something about when they were little. It doesn't have to be fantastic, just something that you've remembered.'

Anderson began to smile and looked up.

'There's summat. It's nowt though.'

'It must be if you remember it.'

'It's daft really.'

'Well tell us then, and let's all have a laugh.'

'Well it was once when I was a kid. I was at Junior school, I think, or somewhere like that, and went down to Fowlers Pond, me and this other kid. Reggie Clay they called him, he didn't come to this school; he flitted and went away somewhere. Anyway it was Spring, tadpole time, and it's swarming with tadpoles down there in Spring. Edges of t'pond are all black with 'em, and me and this other kid started to catch 'em. It was easy, all you did, you just put your hands together and scooped a handful of water up and you'd got a handful of tadpoles. Anyway we were mucking about with 'em, picking 'em up and chucking 'em back and things, and we were on about taking some home, but we'd no jam jars. So this kid, Reggie, says, "Take thi wellingtons off and put some in there, they'll be all right 'til tha gets home." So I took 'em off and we put some water in 'em and then we started to put taddies in 'em. We kept ladling 'em in and I says to this kid, "Let's have a competition, thee have one welli' and I'll have t'other, and we'll see who can get most in!" So he started to fill one welli' and I started to fill t'other. We must have been at it hours, and they got thicker and thicker, until at t'end there was no water left in 'em, they were just jam packed wi'taddies.

'You ought to have seen 'em, all black and shiny, right up to t'top. When we'd finished we kept dipping us fingers into 'em and whipping 'em up at each other, all shouting and excited like. Then this kid says to me, "I bet tha daren't put one on." And I says, "I bet tha daren't." So we said we'd put one on each. We wouldn't though, we kept reckoning to, then running away, so we tossed up and him who lost had to do it first. And I lost, oh, and you'd to take your socks off an' all. So I took my socks off, and I kept looking at this welli' full of taddies, and this kid kept saying, "Go on then, tha frightened, tha frightened." I was an' all. Anyway I shut my eyes and started to put my foot in. Oooo. It was just like putting your feet into live jelly. They were frozen. And when my foot went down, they all came over t'top of my wellington, and when I got my foot to t'bottom, I could feel 'em all squashing about between my toes.

'Anyway I'd done it, and I says to this kid, "Thee put thine on now." But he wouldn't, he was dead scared, so I put it on instead. I'd got used to it then, it was all right after a bit; it sent your legs all excited and tingling like. When I'd got 'em both on I started to walk up to this kid, waving my arms and making spook noises; and as I walked they all came squelching over t'tops again and ran down t'sides. This kid looked frightened to death, he kept looking down at my wellies so I tried to run at him and they all spurted up my legs. You ought to have seen him. He just screamed out and ran home roaring.

'It was a funny feeling though when he'd gone; all quiet, with nobody there, and up to t'knees in tadpoles.'

Silence. The class up to their knees in tadpoles. Mr Farthing allowed them a pause for assimilation. Then, before their involvement could disintegrate into local gossip, he used it to try to inspire an emulator.

'Very good, Anderson. Thank you. Now has anyone else anything interesting to tell us?'

No hands went up.

'No? What about you, Casper?'

Billy was bending over, inspecting his hands under cover of the desk. Pink weals were stamped across his fingertips. When he opened his fingers the weals broke into segments; each segment resembling a bump of nettle-rash. He blew on them, and cooled them with his tongue.

'Casper!'

Billy sat up and put his hands away.

'What, Sir?'

'What, Sir. You'd know if you'd been listening. Have you been listening'

'Yes, Sir.'

'Tell me what we've been talking about then.'

'Er ... stories, Sir.'

'What kind of stories?'

'Er ...'

'You don't know, do you?'

'No, Sir.'

'He's been asleep again, Sir!'

Billy scraped his chair round and shouted above the laughter:

'Thee shut thi mouth, Tibby!'

'Casper! Tibbut! You'll both be asleep in a minute. I'll knock you to sleep! The rest of you – Q U I E T.'

He slid off the desk edge and took one step down the nearest aisle. The result – quiet.

'You haven't heard a word of what's been said, have you, Casper?'

'Yes, Sir – some of it.'

'Some of it. I'll bet you have. Stand up, lad.'

Billy sighed and pushed the chair away with the backs of his knees.

'Right, now you can do some work for a change. You're going to tell us any story about yourself, the same as Anderson did.'

'I don't know any, Sir.'

'Well you can just stand there until you do.'

Mr Farthing began to pace across the space between the board and the desk.

'There's always somebody to spoil it. There's always someone you can't suit, who has to be awkward, who refuses to be interested in anything, someone like you, Casper.'

He pivoted round on one foot and thrust an arm out at Billy.

'I'm giving you two minutes to think of something lad, and if you haven't started then, the whole class is coming back at four!'

There was a general stiffening of backs and looking round wide-eyed, accompanied by grumbling and interspersed with eh's and threatening encouragements.

'Come on, Billy.'

' 'Else tha dies.'

'Say owt.'

'If I've to come back I'll kill him.'

Billy tried to blink back the tears shining in his eyes.

'I'm waiting, Casper.'

Mr Farthing sat down and nudged back his jacket sleeve to look at his watch.

'We haven't got all day, Casper.'

'Tell him about thi hawk, Billy.'

'If anyone else calls out, it will be the last call he'll make! ... What hawk, Casper? ... Casper, I'm speaking to you.'

Billy continued to show Mr Farthing the top of his head.

'Look this way boy when I'm speaking to you.'

Billy looked up slowly.

'And stop sulking just because somebody says a few words to you! ... Now then, what's this about this hawk? What is it, a stuffed one?'

The shout of laughter from the class spilled the first tears on to Billy's face, and left Mr Farthing looking about in surprise at these opposing reactions to his question.

'What's funny about that?'

Tibbut half stood up, placing the weight of his body on the desk top as he shot one arm up.

'Well, Tibbut?'

'He's got a hawk, Sir. It's a kestrel. He's mad about it. He never knocks about wi' anybody else now, he just looks after this hawk all t'time. He's crackers wi' it!'

Billy turned on him, the movement releasing a fresh head of tears into wobbly halting motion down his cheeks.

'It's better than thee anyday, Tibby!'

'I told you, Sir, he goes daft if you say owt about it.'

'Right, Casper, sit down.'

Billy sat down and wiped his cheeks on the shoulders of his

jacket. Mr Farthing rested his elbows on his desk and tapped his teeth with his thumb nails, waiting for Billy to collect himself.

'Now then, Billy, tell me about this hawk. Where did you get it from?'

'Found it.'

'Where?'

'In t'wood.'

'What had happened to it? Was it injured or something?'

'It was a young 'un. It must have tumbled from a nest.'

'And how long have you had it?'

'Since last year.'

'All that time? Where do you keep it?'

'In a shed.'

'And what do you feed it on?'

'Beef. Mice. Birds.'

'Isn't it cruel though, keeping it in a shed all the time? Wouldn't it be happier flying free?'

Billy looked at Mr Farthing for the first time since he had told him to sit down.

'I don't keep it in t'shed all t'time. I fly it every day.'

'And doesn't it fly away? I thought hawks were wild birds.'

'' Course it don't fly away. I've trained it.'

Billy looked round, as though daring anyone to challenge this authority.

'Trained it? I thought you'd to be an expert to train hawks.'

'Well I did it.'

'Was it difficult?'

'' Course it was. You've to be right ... right patient wi' 'em and take your time.'

'Well tell me how you did it then. I've never met a falconer before, I suppose I must be in select company.'

Billy hutched his chair up and leaned forward over his desk.

'Well what you do is, you train 'em through their stomachs. You can only do owt wi' 'em when they're hungry, so you do all your training at feeding time.

'I started training Kes after I'd had her about a fortnight, when she was hard penned, that means her tail feathers and

64

wing feathers had gone hard at their bases. You have to use a torch at night and keep inspecting 'em. It's easy if you're quiet, you just go up to her as she's roosting, and spread her tail and wings. If t'feathers are blue near t'bottom o' t'shaft, that means there's blood in 'em an' they're still soft, so they're not ready yet. When they're white and hard then they're ready, an' you can start training her then.

'Kes wa' as fat as a pig though at first. All young hawks are when you first start to train 'em, and you can't do much wi' 'em 'til you've got their weight down. You've to be ever so careful though, you don't just starve 'em, you weigh 'em before every meal and gradually cut their food down, 'til you go in one time an' she's keen, an' that's when you start getting somewhere. I could tell wi' Kes, she jumped straight on my glove as I held it towards her. So while she wa' feeding I got hold of her jesses an' ...'

'Her what?'

'Jesses.'

'Jesses. How do you spell that?'

Mr Farthing stood up and stepped back to the board.

'Er, J-E-S-S-E-S.'

As Billy enunciated each letter, Mr Farthing linked them together on the blackboard.

'Jesses. And what are jesses, Billy?'

'They're little leather straps that you fasten round its legs as soon as you get it. She wears these all t'time, and you get hold of 'em when she sits on your glove. You push your swivel through ...'

'Whoa! Whoa!'

Mr Farthing held up his hands as though Billy was galloping towards him.

'You'd better come out here and give us a demonstration. We're not all experts you know.'

Billy stood up and walked out, taking up position at the side of Mr Farthing's desk. Mr Farthing reared his chair on to its back legs, swivelled it sideways on one leg, then lowered it on to all fours facing Billy.

'Right, off you go.'

'Well when she stands on your fist, you pull her jesses down between your fingers.'

Billy held his left fist out and drew the jesses down between his first and second fingers.

'Then you get your swivel, like a swivel on a dog lead, press both jesses together, and thread 'em through t'top ring of it. T'jesses have little slits in 'em near t'bottom, like buttonholes in braces, and when you've got t'jesses through t'top ring o' t'swivel, you open these slits with your finger, and push t' bottom ring through, just like fastening a button.'

With the swivel now attached to the jesses, Billy turned to Mr Farthing.

'Do you see?'

'Yes, I see. Carry on.'

'Well when you've done that, you thread your leash, that's a leather thong, through t'bottom ring o' t'swivel ...'

Billy carefully threaded the leash, grabbed the loose end as it penetrated the ring, and pulled it through.

'... until it binds on t'knot at t'other end. Have you got that?'

'Yes, I think so. Just let me get it right. The jesses round the hawk's legs are attached to a swivel, which is then attached to a lead ...'

'A leash!'

'Leash, sorry. Then what?'

'You wrap your leash round your fingers and tie it on to your little finger.'

'So that the hawk is now attached to your hand?'

'That's right. Well when you've reached this stage and it's stepping on to your glove regular, and feeding all right and not bating too much ...'

'Bating? What's that?'

'Trying to fly off; in a panic like.'

'How do you spell it?'

'B-A-T-I-N-G.'

'Carry on.'

'Well when you've reached this stage inside, you can try feeding her outside and getting her used to other things. You

66

call this manning. That means taming, and you've got to have her well manned before you can start training her right.'

While Billy was talking Mr Farthing reached out and slowly printed on the board B A T I N G; watching Billy all the time as though he was a hawk, and that any sudden movement, or rasp of chalk would make him bate from the side of the desk.

'You take her out at night first and don't go near anybody. I used to walk her round t'fields at t'back of our house at first, then as she got less nervous I started to bring her out in t'day and then take her near other folks, and dogs and cats and cars and things. You've to be ever so careful when you're outside though, 'cos hawks are right nervous and they've got fantastic eyesight, and things are ten times worse for them than they are for us. So you've to be right patient, an' all t'time you're walking her you've to talk to her, all soft like, like you do to a baby.'

He paused for breath. Mr Farthing nodded him on before he had time to become self-conscious.

'Well when you've manned her, you can start training her right then. You can tell when she's ready 'cos she looks forward to you comin' an' there's no trouble gettin' her on to your glove. Not like at first when she's bating all t'time.

'You start inside first, makin' her jump on to your glove for her meat. Only a little jump at first, then a bit further and so on; and every time she comes you've to give her a scrap o' meat. A reward like. When she'll come about a leash length straight away, you can try her outside, off a fence post or summat like that. You put her down, hold on to t'end of your leash wi' your right hand, and hold your glove out for her to fly to. This way you can get a double leash length. After she's done this, you can take her leash off an' attach a creance in its place.'

'Creance?'

Mr Farthing leaned over to the blackboard.

'C-R-E-A-N-C-E – it's a long line, I used a long nylon fishing line wi' a clasp off a dog lead, tied to one end. Well you clip this to your swivel, pull your leash out, and put your hawk down on a fence post. Then you walk away into t'field unwindin' your creance, an' t'hawk sits there waitin' for you to stop an' hold your glove up. It's so it can't fly away, you see.'

'Yes I see. It all sounds very skilful and complicated, Billy.'

'It don't sound half as bad as it is though. I've just telled you in a couple o' minutes how to carry on, but it takes weeks to go through all them stages. They're as stubborn as mules, hawks, they're right tempr ... tempr ...'

'Temperamental.'

'Temperamental. Sometimes she'd be all right, then next time I'd go in, she'd go mad, screamin' an' batin' as though she'd never seen me before. You'd think you'd learnt her summat, an' put her away feelin' champion, then t'next time you went you were back where you started. You just couldn't reckon it up at all.'

He looked down at Mr Farthing, eyes animated, cheeks flushed under a wash of smeared tears and dirt.

'You make it sound very exciting though.'

'It is, Sir. But most exciting thing wa' when I flew her free first time. You ought to have been there then. I wa' frightened to death.'

Mr Farthing turned to the class, rotating his trunk without moving his chair.

'Do you want to hear about it?'

Chorus: 'Yes, Sir.'

Mr Farthing smiled and turned back to Billy.

'Carry on, Casper.'

'Well I'd been flyin' it on t'creance for about a week, an' it was' comin' to me owt up to thirty, forty yards, an' it says in t'books that when it's comin' this far, straight away, it's ready to fly loose. I daren't though. I kept sayin' to missen, I'll just use t'creance today to make sure, then I'll fly it free tomorrow. But when tomorrow came I did t'smack same thing. I did this for about four days an' I got right mad wi' missen 'cos I knew I'd have to do it sometime. So on t'last day I didn't feed her up, just to make sure that she'd be sharp set next morning. I hardly went to sleep that night, I wa' thinking about it that much.

'It wa' one Friday night, an' when I got up next morning I thought right, if she flies off, she flies off, an' it can't be helped. So I went down to t'shed. She wa' dead keen an' all, walking about on her shelf behind t'bars, an' screamin' out when she saw me comin'. So I took her out in t'field and tried her on t'creance first time, an' she came like a rocket. So I thought, right, this time.

'I unclipped t'creance, took t'swivel off an' let her hop on to t'fence post. There was nowt stoppin' her now, she wa' just standin' there wi' her jesses on. She could have took off an' there wa' nowt I could have done about it. I wa' terrified. I thought she's forced to go, she's forced to, she'll just fly off an' that'll be it. But she didn't. She just sat there looking round while I backed off into t'field. I went right into t'middle, then held my glove up an' shouted her.'

Billy held his left fist up and stared out of the window.

'Come on, Kes! Come on then! Nowt happened at first, then, just when I wa' going' to walk back to her, she came. You ought to have seen her. Straight as a die, about a yard off t'floor. An' t'speed! She came twice as fast as when she had t'creance on, 'cos it used to drag in t'grass an' slow her down. She came like lightnin', head dead still, an' her wings never made a sound, then wham! Straight up on to t'glove, claws out grabbin' for t'meat,' simultaneously demonstrating the last yard of her flight with his right hand, gliding it towards, then slapping it down on his raised fist.

'I wa' that pleased I didn't know what to do wi' missen, so I thought just to prove it, I'll try her again, an' she came t'second time just as good. Well that was it. I'd done it. I'd trained her.'

'Well done, Billy.'

'It wa' a smashin' feeling. You can't believe that you'll be able to do it. Not when you first get one, or when you see 'em wild. They seem that fierce, an' . . . an' wild.'

'And was that the end of it then?'

'More or less, Sir. After that I introduced her to t'lure; that's a leather weight tied on t'end of a cord. You tie meat on to it and swing it round and she flies round an' keeps stoopin' for it.'

'Yes, yes. I remember a falconer once demonstrating it on television. He swung it round in a similar fashion to a bolus, and each time the hawk swooped in, he swung it down and kept it just out of its reach. The donkey and the carrot principle.'

'That's right. You fly 'em to a lure to keep 'em fit. An' that's as far as you can go wi' a kestrel. You can't catch owt wi' 'em, but you train 'em smack same as other hawks. Only difference is, that after you've introduced other hawks to t'lure, you can enter 'em at game.'

'Tell me something. Is it difficult, swinging this lure?'

'It is at first. It's murder. You can't judge t'swing right, t'hawk don't know what it's supposed to do, an' you just finish up wi' it all wrapped round you, else hitting t'hawk in t'chest or summat. It's a right pantomime 'til you get used to it.'

Mr Farthing set up a series of nodded agreements.

'Yes, yes. I suspected as much when he made it look so simple.'

'It's not, Sir.'

'But then that's the mark of an expert, isn't it? Someone who makes a difficult skill look easy?'

'Yes, Sir.'

'And makes us think that we can all do it. Which we can't, of course.'

He shook his head, and Billy confirmed his doubts.

'No, Sir.'

'Right you can sit down now. That was very good, I enjoyed it, and I'm sure the class did.'

Billy blushed then walked back to his place, looking down at his feet. His return to the ranks was greeted by a splatter of applause, which Mr Farthing allowed to run its natural course.

'Right. We've just heard two excellent accounts, one from Anderson about his tadpoles, the other from Casper about his hawk. Both these accounts were true, they happened, so we call them ...?

He looped a forefinger vaguely over the class, waiting for the correct answer to draw it, and halt its peregrinations.

'Facts, Sir.'

The finger zipped horizontally from the corridor side of the room to the window side, and stopped, pointing into the centre of the row.

'Right, facts. Factual accounts. True stories. Now then 4c, what's the opposite of fact? What do we call stories that are imaginary?'

He hooked a thumb over his shoulder at the board.

Chorus : 'Fiction, Sir!'

'Right, fiction. Just look it up in your dictionaries to make sure. First one to find it gets a house point.'

There was a whizzing of pages to localize F, followed by a more deliberate turning of odd pages, and a final pointing of forefingers.

'Sir!'

'Right, Whitbread. Read it out.'

'Fiction. Inven-ted state-ment or narra-tive, novels, stories collectiv, collectiv-ely collectively; Blimey.' 'Go on, have a go at it, lad.' 'Convent, convent-ion-ally, I know, conventionally accepted false-hood. Fic-tit-ious, fictitious, not genuine, imagin-ary, assumed.'

'Good. Have you all found it now?'

They had all found it while Whitbread was reading the definition, and there was silence while they confirmed it mentally.

'Have you all got that? Fiction; invented statement, novels, stories, falsehood, not genuine, imaginary, assumed. All right?' There was no response so he assumed that they were.

'Right, now close your dictionaries and listen carefully ... You're now going to write me a piece of fiction. That is, any imaginary story, as opposed to Anderson's and Casper's stories, which were true or factual. I don't care what you write about as long as it's fictitious, and to make sure that it is, and so that you can really get your imaginations working and let yourself go at it, we'll call it ...'

He stood up and turned to the board, and announced each word of the title as he printed it:

'A TALL STORY'

He placed the chalk back in its groove and blew some dust off his fingers.

'You know what a tall story is, don't you? Anybody doesn't?' Everybody glanced round, but no hands went up.

'Tell us then, Jordan.'

'It's summat that's too far-fetched to be true.'

'Good. Something that is unbelievable, or far-fetched as you call it. For example, if I said to Casper, 'Why were you late this morning?" ...'

'I wasn't late this morning, Sir.'

Mr Farthing looked at the ceiling and laughed out. He startled some of the boys into laughing at him. Then, still smiling, he lowered his face and continued.

'That would be the perfect tall story, Casper.'

Billy just looked at him and nobody laughed.

'Right, forget it. If I said to Casper, "Why were you late this morning?" and he replied, "Well when I got up this morning our house had been washed out to sea, so I caught the 8.30 whale to shore, and hitched a lift on an eagle's back. But we were held up for twenty minutes in a bird-jam, and that's why I was late." Well if Casper came to me with that tale, I'd probably look at him and say, "That's a bit of a tall story, isn't it, lad?"'

'It would be an' all, Sir.'

'You're right, Jordan, it would. Have you all got the idea now? Right then, you,' pointing at them, 'tell me,' pointing at himself, 'a tall story. B U T, and get this, I want no repeats of the story I've just told. That was just an example, so forget it, and let's see what you can produce on your own.

'Jordan, give the books out. Whitbread, pens. Tibbut, pencils, Mann, rulers.'

While the books and pens and pencils and rulers were being distributed, Mr Farthing appended the date to the title on the board.

'Underline your last piece of work and leave a line before you write the title. And don't forget your margins.'

He sat down to direct the scene; and gradually, after new nibs had been fitted, pencils sharpened, rubbers borrowed and returned, margins ruled, inkwells filled, blotters blotted, inquiries answered, arguments settled, boys admonished, monitors seated, pens, pencils, rulers, blotters, books dropped and retrieved, the class settled to work.

Billy dipped his nib right up to the metal holder, then, balancing on the front legs of his chair, book and head askew, he began his story:

A tall story

One day I wolke up and my muther said to me heer Billy theres your brecfast in bed for you there was backen and egg and bred and butter and a big pot of tea when I had my brekfast the sun was shining out side and I got drest and whent down stairs we lived in a big hous up moor edge and we add carpits on the stairs and in the all and sentrall eeting. When I got down I said wers are Jud his goind the army my muther saide and hees not coming back. but your dades coming back in sted. there was a big fire in the room and my dad came in caring his cas that he tulke a way with him I havent seen him for a long time but he was just the sam as he went away I was glad hed come back and are Jud had gon away when I got to school all the teacherr were good to me they said allow Billy awo you gowing on and they all pated me on the head and smilled and we did interesting things all day.when I got home my muther saide I not gowing to work eny more and we all had chips beans for awur tea then we got redy and we all went to the picturs we went up stairs and had Ice cream at the intervells and then we all went home and had fish and chips for awur super and then we went to bed.

At break Billy went out into the yard. The wind, cutting straight across from the playing fields, made him turn his back and raise a shoulder while he looked round for a sheltered place. All the corners were occupied. Boys lounged along the walls and window ledges, singly, in pairs, and in groups. Their conversation was mostly quiet, their movements spasmodic; a shift of stance, a warming burst, or the sudden milling of a group, as one of its members moved and tried to use another as a windbreak. But these boys were spectators. Most of the noise and movement came from the expanses of the yard where hundreds of boys were in action. Walking and talking, chasing and dodging, making thoroughfares of football matches and other ball games. Wrestling and riding, and in the smaller pockets of space playing less strenuous games of concentration, using smaller objects. All intermingling, the patterns of play in a state of flux round occasional boys standing stock still amongst it all. Beneath their feet, their reflections flashed as dark patches in the wet concrete, which reflected the shifting grey and black of the low sky.

And above them all the noise: combinations of object and voice, depending on chance, and on the emotions of each child involved in each activity at a given time. Sometimes heightening, sometimes faltering, but the incidents causing these fluctuations in volume and pitch impossible to locate within the general activity.

The noise: spreading from the yard across the estate, but leaving the bulk of its volume behind, so that people all over the estate, on the streets and in their gardens, on hearing it looked up towards its source, as though expecting it to be visible above the rooftops like a cloud, or the rising sun.

Billy walked round to the back of the school and crossed the strip of asphalt to the cycle shed. Look-outs were posted at either end of the shed, and in one corner a gang of boys was assembled; some smoking, some hanging around in the hope of a smoke. The three smokers were hanging around. So was Mac-Dowall.

'Got owt, Casper?'

Billy shook his head.

'Tha never has, thee. Tha just cadges all thine. Casper the cadger, that's what they ought to call thee.'

'I wouldn't gi' thee owt if I had, MacDowall.'

'I'll gi' thee summat in a minute.'

Billy crossed in front of the row of bicycles parked with their front wheels slotted into concrete blocks. One machine was mounted, the rider backpedalling vacantly, as though waiting to be snapped by a seaside photographer. Billy leaned on the corrugated tin wall at the other end of the shed and looked out across the asphalt. Directly opposite was the door of the boiler house. At one side of the door were eight dustbins in a line, and at the other side, a heap of coke. The door was painted green.

'What's tha gone over there for, Casper, frightened?'

Billy ignored him and continued to stare out. MacDowall, pinching a tab between his middle finger and thumb nails, twitched his head in Billy's direction.

'Come on, lads, let's go and keep him company.'

Grinning, he led the line of smokers across the shed, and they took up position in the corner, behind Billy. Billy half turned, so that his back was against the tin, and the gang were down one side of him.

'What's up, Casper, don't tha like company?'

He winked at the boys around him.

'They say thi mother does.'

The gang began to snigger and snuggle into each other. Billy turned his back on them again.

'I've heard tha's got more uncles than any kid in this city.'

The shout of laughter seemed to jerk Billy round as though it had pulled him by the shoulder.

'Shut thi mouth! Shut it can't tha!'

'Come and make me.'

'Tha can only pick on little kids. Tha daren't pick on anybody thi own size!'

'Who daren't?'

'Thee! Tha wouldn't say what tha's just said to our Jud. He'd murder thi.'

'I'm not frightened of him.'

'Tha would be if he wa' here.'

'Would I heck, he's nowt, your Jud.'

'Tha what! He's t'cock o' t'estate, that's all.'

'Who says? I bet I know somebody who can fight him.'

'Who? . . . thi father?'

The gang laughed and began to fan out behind MacDowall. MacDowall was furious.

'Your Jud wouldn't stick up for thee, anyroad. He isn't even thi brother.'

'What is he then, my sister?'

'He's not thi right brother, my mother says. They don't even call him Casper for a start.'

'Course he's my brother! We live in t'same house, don't we?'

75

'An' he don't look a bit like thee, he's twice as big for a start. You're nowt like brothers.'

'I'm tellin' him! I'm tellin' him what tha says, MacDowall!'

Billy ran at him. The gang scattered. MacDowall took a step back, lifted one knee, and pushed Billy off with his foot. Billy came back at him. MacDowall delivered a straight right, which caught Billy smack in the chest and bounced him back on to his arse.

'Get away, you little squirt, before I spit on thi an' drown thi.'

Billy got up, coughing and crying and rubbing his chest. He stood at a distance glancing round, his fingers clenching and unclenching. Then he turned and ran out of the shed, across the asphalt to the pile of coke. He scooped up two handfuls, then, cupping this stock to his chest with his left hand, he began to throw it lump by lump into the shed. MacDowall turned his back and hunched his shoulders. The others scattered, knocking bicycles off balance and sending them toppling against other bicycles, which leaned over and swayed under the weight. The coke clattered against the tin with such rapidity that the vibrations produced by each clatter were linked together into a continual ring. One lump hit MacDowall in the back, another on the leg. He cursed Billy and began to back out, peeping over his raised left arm. Then, as Billy stooped for fresh ammunition, panting and pausing for a moment's rest, MacDowall straightened up and ran at him. Billy turned at the footsteps, threw and missed, then tried to escape up the coke, his pumps sinking out of sight at every step. MacDowall reached the bottom of the heap at full speed, and with his feet pushing off firm ground, dived and landed full length on Billy's back. The coke scrunched, and the lumps were ground together and moulded into shifting waves under the weight.

'Fight! Fight!'

The news was relayed round to the yard, and within seconds the swirling pattern of activity changed to a linear form as boys abandoned their games and raced round to the back of the school. Billy and MacDowall had rolled the peak of the coalheap into a plateau, and gradually, as more and more spectators arrived, the first arrivals were forced up the heap, and the coke was trampled backwards and levelled out across the asphalt. Latecomers climbed on to the dustbins, three and four to a lid, encircling each other's bodies with their arms to maintain balance. Sometimes they overbalanced and toppled off into a shouting heap, grabbing and banging the occupants of the next bin, so that periodically whole bunches of boys were knocked over like a row of dominoes. To be replaced by fresh spectators; who in turn were pulled down by the legs, by the first fallen.

MacDowall was now astride Billy, pinning his biceps under his knees. The encircling crowd was directly over them, their heads outlining a rough spotlight, their bodies and legs the beam, as they strained outwards against the pressure from behind. Individual cries of encouragement were distinguishable amongst the medley and the perpetual grinding of coke, and round the outskirts other skirmishes were developing, forming sideshows to the the main attraction.

Enter Mr Farthing, running. The boys mooching around the fringes of the fight, like supporters locked out of a football ground, spread the word. The word spread amongst the back ranks of the crowd, and the knot slackened as boys hurried away before Mr Farthing could reach them. But at the core of the activity the attention was too fixed to be diverted, and when Mr Farthing forced his way through, dragging boys aside by their arms, their faces turned on him, flicking through the emotions of anger, shock, and finally amusement at the thought of their initial reaction. He lifted MacDowall off Billy and shook him like a terrier shakes a rat. The cokes were vacated and the spectators adjourned to a safer distance. Mr Farthing looked round at them, blazing.

'I'm giving you lot ten seconds to get back to the yard. If I see one face after that time I'll give its owner the biggest belting he's ever received.'

He started to count. Four seconds later MacDowall's and Billy's faces were the only two in sight.

'Now then what's going off.'

Billy began to cry. MacDowall wiped his nose along the back of one hand and looked down at it.

'Well? . . . Casper?'

'It wa' him, Sir! He started it!'

'I didn't, Sir! It wa' him, he started chucking cokes at me!'

'Ar, what for though?'

'Nowt!'

'You liar!'

Mr Farthing closed his eyes and cancelled all the explanations with a crossed sweep of his arms.

'Shut up. Both of you. It's the same old tale; it's nobody's fault, and nobody started it, you just happened to be fighting on top of a heap of coke for no reason at all. I ought to send you both to Mr Gryce!'

He tossed his head back at the school, and the words came out, ground from between his teeth.

'Just look at the mess you've made!'

Two dustbins were lying on their sides, their contents spilling out, and three more bins were without their lids. The pile of coke had been trampled into a cokey beach, and odd lumps had been kicked across the asphalt, some into the cycle shed.

'Just look at it! It's disgusting! And just look at the state of you both!'

One lap of MacDowall's shirt curved out from beneath his sweater, and covered one thigh, like half an apron. Billy's shirt buttons had burst open all down the front. One button was missing, the corresponding button-hole ripped open. Their hair looked as though they had been scratching their scalps solidly for a week, and their faces were the colour of colliers'.

'And stop blubbering, Casper! You're not dying, lad!'

'He will be when I get hold of him.'

Mr Farthing stepped up to MacDowall and bent his knees to bring their faces level.

'You're a brave boyo, aren't you, MacDowall? He's just about your size isn't he, Casper? Well if you're so keen on fighting, why don't you pick on somebody your own size? Eh? Eh?' simultaneously pushing MacDowall twice in the shoulder.

'Because you're scared, aren't you? Aren't you, MacDowall?' Right jab, right again, stepping up each time MacDowall retreated.

'You're nothing but a bully boy. The classic example of a bully! If it isn't Casper, then it's someone else like him. Isn't it, isn't it, MacDowall?' Jab. Jab.

They left Billy behind, progressing into the shed with halting corresponding steps, like partners learning to dance.

'What would you say if I pinned you to the floor and smacked you across the face?' Jab. Jab.

MacDowall began to sob.

'You'd say I was a bully, wouldn't you lad? And you'd be right, because I'm bigger and stronger, and I know that I could beat you to pulp before we started. Just like you know, Mac-Dowall, with every boy you pick on!' The next two jabs developed into thumps.

'I'll tell my dad!'

'Of course you will, lad. Boys like you always tell their dads. And then do you know what I'll do, MacDowall? I'll tell mine. And then what will happen? Eh?'

MacDowall banged the back of his head on the back of the shed, making the tin rattle. Mr Farthing completed his last step, closing the gap between them again.

'And do you know, MacDowall, that my dad's the heavy-weight champion of the world? So what's going to happen to your dad then. Eh? And what's going to happen to you? Eh? Eh? MacDowall?'

He roared out this last question and stood up straight, dragging MacDowall up by the lapels to keep their faces level. MacDowall was now blubbering freely.

'Well, what's it like to be bullied? You don't like it much, do you?'

He dropped MacDowall and pushed him hard against the tin.

'And you'll like it even less if I ever catch you at it again.'

He enunciated this warning slowly and carefully, as though MacDowall was a foreigner, having difficulty with the language.

'U N D E R S T A N D?'

'Yes, Sir.'

'Good. Now get into school, get cleaned up and ... wait a minute, I've got your form next, haven't I?'

'Yes, Sir.'

'Right then, you can spend it shovelling that lot back into shape.'

He pivoted on his left foot and toe-ended a lump of coke back across the asphalt. It cannoned into other lumps, then took its place amongst the spread. A glance away and it was lost.

'And when I come out at twelve o'clock I want every lump back in its place. Right?'

'Yes, Sir.'

'Right. Get cracking.'

MacDowall walked away, rubbing his eyes and his cheeks with his knuckles and the backs of his hands. He stopped rubbing them to glance at Billy as he passed. Mr Farthing followed him slowly out of the shed, timing his confrontation with Billy to coincide with the disappearance of MacDowall round the corner of the building.

'Now then, Casper, what's it all about?'

Billy shook his head.

'What do you mean?' ... Mr Farthing mimicked him. 'It must have been something.'

'O ... I can't tell you right, Sir.'

'Why can't you?'

"Cos I can't. I can't, Sir!'

The skin on his face tightened, pulling at his mouth and his eyes, and he began to cry again.

'He started calling me names an' sayin' things about my dad an' my mother an' our Jud, an' everybody wa' laughin', an' ...'

His sobs became so violent that they impaired his breathing and interrupted his speech. Mr Farthing held up one hand, nodding.

'All right, lad, calm down. It's finished with now.'

He waited for him to calm down, then shook his head slowly.

'I don't know, you always seem to cop it, don't you, Casper?'

Billy stood with his head bowed, sniffing quietly to himself.

'I wonder why? Why do you think it is?'

'What, Sir?'

'That you're always in trouble?'

"Cos everybody picks on me, that's why.'

He looked up with such intensity that his eyes and the tears webbed in the lower lashes seemed to fuse and shine like lumps of crystal. Mr Farthing looked away to hide a smile.

'Yes I know they do, but why?'

'I don't know, they just do, that's all.'

'Perhaps it's because you're a bad lad.'

'P'raps I am, sometimes. But I'm not that bad, I'm no worse than stacks o' kids, but they just seem to get away with it.'

'You think you're just unlucky, then?'

'I don't know, Sir. I seem to get into bother for nowt. You know, for daft things, like this morning in t'hall. I wasn't doin' owt, I just dozed off that's all. I wa' dog tired, I'd been up since six, then I'd to run round wi' t'papers, then run home to have a look at t'hawk, then run to school. We', I mean, you'd be tired wouldn't you, Sir?'

Mr Farthing chuckled.

'I'd be exhausted.'

'That's nowt to get t'stick for, is it Sir, being tired? You can't tell Gryce ... Mr Gryce though, he'd kill you! Do you know, Sir, there wa' a kid this morning stood outside his room wi' us, he'd only brought a message from another teacher, and Mr Gryce gave him t'stick!'

Mr Farthing's face broadened into a grin, and his mouth broke open, laughing. Billy watched these changes in expression seriously.

'It's all right for you, Sir. What about that kid though, he was as sick as a dog after.'

Mr Farthing immediately became serious again.

'You're right, lad, it's not funny. It was just the way you told it, that's all.'

'An' this morning in English, when I wasn't listening. It wasn't that I wasn't bothered, it wa' my hands, they were killin' me! You can't concentrate when your hands are stingin' like mad!'

'No, I don't suppose you can.'

'I still got into trouble for it though, didn't I?'

'You made up for it though, didn't you?'

'I know, but it's allus like that though.'

'What is?'

'Teachers. They never think it might be their fault an' all.'

'No, I don't think many do, lad.'

'They think they're right every time. But there's sometimes when you can't help it, like this morning; an' like when you get thumped for not listenin' when it's dead boring. We', I mean, you can't help not listenin' when it's not interestin', can you, Sir?'

'No you can't, Casper.'

'You daren't say that to t'teachers though, they'd say, "Don't be insolent boy," smack!'

Billy stood up straight and waggled his head about, looking stern. Then he smacked the space between Mr Farthing and himself. Mr Farthing laughed out at his impersonation.

'That's what they'd say though, Sir.'

'I'm not saying it and I'm a teacher, aren't I?'

'Ar, well ...'

'Well what?'

'You do at least try to learn us summat, most o' t'others don't. They're not bothered about us, just because we're in 4C, you can tell, they talk to us like muck. They're allus callin' us idiots, an' numbskulls, an' cretins, an' looking at their watches to see how long it is to t'end o' t'lesson. They're fed up wi' us. We're fed up wi' them, then when there's any trouble, they pick on me 'cos I'm t'littlest.'

'They're not all like that, surely?'

'Most of 'em, Sir. An', anyway ... I can talk to you better than most folks.'

He looked down, blushing. Mr Farthing looked down at the top of his head.

'How are things at home these days?'

'All right, Sir. Same as usual I suppose.'

'What about the police? Have you been in trouble with them lately?'

'No, Sir.'

'Because you've reformed? Or because you haven't been caught?'

'I've reformed, Sir.'

Mr Farthing smiled at him. But Billy was serious.

'It's right, Sir, I haven't done owt for ages now! That's one o' t'reasons why MacDowall's allus pickin' on me, 'cos I don't knock about wi' their gang any more. An' it's since I stopped goin' wi' them that I stopped gettin' into trouble.'

'What happened, did you have an argument or something?'

'No, Sir, it wa' when I got my hawk. I got that interested in it that it seemed to take all my time up. It wa' summer then, you see, and I used to take it down our fields at nights. Then when t'dark nights came back, I never got back in wi' 'em. I wasn't bothered any more.

'I try to get hold of falconry books an' read up about 'em now. I make new jesses an' things an' all, an' sometimes I go down to t'shed an' sit wi' a candle lit. It's all right in there. I've got a little paraffin stove that I found, an' it gets right warm, an' we just sit there. It makes you feel right cosy an' snug sat there wi' t'wind blowin' outside.'

'Yes, I'll bet it does.'

'It's stacks better than roamin' t'streets doin' nowt. 'Cos that's all we used to do. Just roam about t'estate muckin' about, fed up to t'teeth an' frozen. I reckon that's why I wa' allus in trouble, we used to break into places an' nick things an' that just for a bit o' excitement. It wa' summat to do, that's all.'

'What about youth clubs? There's one open in this school three evenings a week.'

'I don't like youth clubs. I don't like games. We used to go into t'city, to t'pictures, or to a coffee bar sometimes. But any-road, they can please their sens what they do. I'm not bothered now.'

'You're a lone wolf now then?'

'I'd like to be if only folks'd leave me alone. There's allus somebody after me though. Like this playtime. I only came round to this shed to get out o' t'cold; next thing I know, I'm in a fight. It's same in class. I'm just sittin' there, next news is,

I'm on my feet gettin' t'stick or summat. They're allus sayin' I'm a pest or a nuisance, they talk as though I like gettin' into trouble; but I don't, Sir.

'An 'at home, if owt goes wrong on t'estate, police allus come to our house, even though I've done nowt for ages now. An' they don't believe a word I say! I feel like goin' out an' doin' summat just to spite 'em sometimes.'

'Never mind lad; it'll be all right.'

'Ar, it will that.'

'Just think, you'll be leaving school in a few weeks, starting your first job, meeting fresh people. That's something to look forward to isn't it?'

Billy looked past him without replying.

'Have you got a job yet?'

'No Sir. I've to see t'youth employment bloke this afternoon.'

'What kind of job are you after?'

'I'm not bothered. Owt'll do me.'

'You'll try to get something that interests you though?'

'I shan't have much choice shall I ? I shall have to take what they've got.'

'I thought you'd have been looking forward to leaving.'

'I'm not bothered.'

'I thought you didn't like school.'

'I don't, but that don't mean that I'll like work, does it? Still, I'll get paid for not liking it, that's one thing.'

'Yes. Yes, I suppose it is.'

Mr Farthing shook his head slightly and looked at his watch.

'I might be able to save up an' buy a goshawk then, I've just been readin' about 'em.'

'Well, I shall have to go and blow the whistle, they've had five minutes extra already.'

'Good.'

'What do you mean?'

'It's games next, that means five minutes less.'

'Well you'd better be off then and get cleaned up, or you're going to have no lesson left.'

'That'd be nice. It'll be an hour o'purgatory on that field.'

He walked away, past Mr Farthing towards the corner of

the building. Mr Farthing followed him slowly, then as Billy
reached the corner he called his name. Billy turned round.

'What, Sir?'

'This hawk of yours. I'd like to see it sometime.'

'Yes, Sir.'

'When do you fly it?'

'Dinner times. It gets dark too early at nights.'

'Do you fly it at home?'

'Yes, Sir. In t'fields at t'back of our house.'

'That's Woods Avenue isn't it?'

'Yes, Sir, 124.'

'Right then, I'll be down. That is if I may?'

'Yes, Sir.'

'Good. You've got me really interested in this bird of yours.'

He began to twirl his whistle, which was suspended from
one forefinger on a yellow band. The metal quickly blurred into
a silver circle, the band shading in the area. Billy watched the
yellow disc for a few seconds, then disappeared round the
corner of the building. The shrill of the whistle immediately
obliterated every other sound in the vicinity.

The toilets were empty. Every square inch of the floor was
wet. All the doors of the cubicles had been thrown open, and
in one of the cubicles a cistern whined as it refilled. On the
opposite wall the copper pipe across the top of the urinals
began to dribble, then W H O O S H sheets of water hissed down
to the porcelain into the channel and flowed away parallel
to the pipe above.

Between the cubicles and the urinals, a double row of sinks
ran down the centre of the room, and at the end of the row
was a wastebin overflowing with a few loosely crumpled paper
towels. Like a bag of cream puffs, the amount of space they
occupied was out of all proportion to their volume, and if they
had been screwed up tightly they would have barely filled the
bottom of the bin, leaving plenty of room for the towels littered around the floor and stuck to the tiles like transfers.

A tap had been left running, and its flow was powerful
enough to maintain a whirlpool in the bottom of the sink. Billy

plugged the next sink and ran the hot water, tempering it with cold water and testing it, until the bowl was well filled. He pushed his sleeves up to his elbows and immersed both hands. The level in the bowl rose and the displaced water escaped down the overflow. Billy leaned on his arms, his hands moulded to the shape of the bowl, and as the steam drifted up about his face he closed his eyes and smiled like the Bisto Kid. He bent over the bowl and slowly dipped his face, held it, and made the water boil by blowing into it. He stood up, shaking his face and wiping the water from his eyes, then he lathered his hands from a bottle of liquid soap, and fouled the water by rinsing them. He lathered them again, made an O with the forefinger and thumb of his right hand, and blew gently on the membrane gathered there. It blossomed to a bubble, the spectrum curving in its skin as it left his hand and floated quietly towards the floor. He reached out to take it back. Touched it. Gone. He blew some more, but they came out small, so he let them drift and time their own oblivion. Then out it came, a jewel, hanging heavy in the air. He reached out to catch it. It bounced off the buff of air, then wavered in the suction as he withdrew his hand. He followed it, and as it fell, he placed his hand below it, allowing his hand to fall more slowly than the bubble, so that slowly, very slowly, the bubble fell closer to his hand. Falling, bubble over hand, both falling, until finally the bubble landed gently on the falling palm. Billy eased them to a halt, and stood up, smiling. He tilted his hand and shifted his head to catch the colours from different angles and in different lights, and while he was looking it vanished, leaving him looking at a lathered palm.

He walked into the changing room as clean and shining as a boy down for breakfast on his seaside holidays. The other boys were packed into the aisles between the rows of pegs, their hanging clothes partitioning the room into corridors. Mr Sugden was passing slowly across one end of the room, looking down the corridors and counting the boys as they changed. He was wearing a violet tracksuit. The top was embellished with cloth badges depicting numerous crests and qualifications, and on the breast a white athlete carried the Olympic torch. The legs were tucked into new white football socks, neatly folded at his ankles, and his football boots were polished as black and shiny as the bombs used by assassins in comic strips. The laces binding them had been scrubbed white, and both boots had been fastened identically : two loops of the foot and one of the ankle, and tied in a neat bow under the tab at the back.

He finished counting and rolled a football off the window sill into his hand. The leather was rich with dubbin, and the new orange lace nipped the slit as firmly as a row of surgical stitches. He tossed it up and caught it on the ends of his fingers, then turned round to Billy.

'Skyving again, Casper?'

'No, Sir, Mr Farthing wanted me; he's been talking to me.'

'I bet that was stimulating for him, wasn't it?'

'What does that mean, Sir?'

'The conversation, lad, what do you think it means?'

'No, Sir, that word, stimult ... stimult-ting.'

'Stimulating you fool, S-T-I-M-U-L-A-T-I-N-G, stimulating!'

'Yes, Sir.'

'Well get changed lad, you're two weeks late already!'

He lifted the elastic webbing of one cuff and rotated his fist to look at his watch on the underside of his wrist.

'Some of us want a game even if you don't.'

'I've no kit, Sir.'

Mr Sugden stepped back and slowly looked Billy up and down, his top lip curling.

'Casper, you make me S I C K.'

'S I C K' penetrated the hubbub, which immediately decreased as the boys stopped their own conversations and turned their attention to Mr Sugden and Billy.

'Every lesson it's the same old story, "Please, Sir, I've no kit." '

The boys tittered at his whipped-dog whining impersonation.

'Every lesson for four years! And in all that time you've made no attempt whatsoever to get any kit, you've skyved and scrounged and borrowed and ...'

He tried this lot on one breath, and his ruddy complexion heightened and glowed like a red balloon as he held his breath and fought for another verb.

'... and ... BEG ...' The balloon burst and the pronunciation of the verb disintegrated.

'Why is it that everyone else can get some but you can't?'

'I don't know, Sir. My mother won't buy me any. She says it's a waste of money, especially now that I'm leaving.'

'You haven't been leaving for four years, have you?'

'No, Sir.'

'You could have bought some out of your spending money, couldn't you?'

'I don't like football, Sir.'

'What's that got to do with it?'

'I don't know, Sir. Anyway I don't get enough.'

'Get a job then. I don't ...'

'I've got one, Sir.'

'Well then! You get paid, don't you?'

'Yes, Sir. But I have to gi' it to my mam. I'm still payin' her for my fines, like instalments every week.'

Mr Sugden bounced the ball on Billy's head, compressing his neck into his shoulders.

'Well you should keep out of trouble then, lad, and then ...'

'I haven't been in trouble, Sir, not ...'

'Shut up, lad! Shut up, before you drive me crackers!'

He hit Billy twice with the ball, holding it between both hands as though he was murdering him with a boulder. The rest of the class grinned behind each other's backs, or placed their fingers over their mouths to suppress the laughter gathering there. They watched Mr Sugden rush into his changing room, and began to giggle, stopping immediately he reappeared waving a pair of giant blue drawers.

'Here Casper, get them on!'

He wanged them across the room, and Billy caught them flying over his head, then held them up for inspection as though he was contemplating buying. The class roared. They would have made Billy two suits and an overcoat.

'They'll not fit me, Sir.'

The class roared again and even Billy had to smile. There was only Mr Sugden not amused.

'What are you talking about, lad? You can get them on, can't you?'

'Yes, Sir.'

'Well they fit you then! Now get changed, QUICK.'

Billy found an empty peg and hung his jacket on it. He was immediately enclosed in a tight square as two lines of boys formed up, one on each side of him between the parallel curtains of clothing. He sat down on the long bench covering the shoe racks, and worked his jeans over his pumps. Mr Sugden broke one side of the square and stood over him.

'And you want your underpants and vest off.'

'I don't wear 'em, Sir.'

As he reached up to hang his trousers on the peg, his shirt lap lifted, revealing his bare cheeks, which looked as smooth and boney as two white billiard balls. He stepped into the shorts and pulled them up to his waist. The legs reached halfway down his shins. He pulled the waist up to his neck and his knees just slid into view. Boys pointed at them, shouting and laughing into each other's faces, and other boys who were still changing rushed to the scene, jumping up on the benches or parting the curtains to see through. And at the centre of it all, Billy, like a brave little clown, was busy trying to make them fit, and Sugden was looking at him as though it was his fault for being too small for them.

'Roll them down and don't be so foolish. You're too daft to laugh at, Casper.'

No one else thought so. Billy started to roll them down from his chest, each tuck shortening the legs and gathering the material round his waist in a floppy blue tyre.

'That'll do. Let's have you all out now.'

He opened the door and led them down the corridor and out into the yard. Some boys waited until he had gone, then they took a run and had a good slide up to the door, rotating slowly as they slid, and finishing up facing the way they had come. Those with rubber studs left long black streaks on the tiles. The plastic and nailed leather studs cut through the veneer and scored deep scratches in the vinyl. When they reached the yard, the pad of the rubber studs on the concrete hardly differed from that in the changing room or the corridor, but the clatter produced by the nailed and plastic studs had a hollow, more metallic ring.

The cold caught Billy's breath as he stepped outside. He stopped dead, glanced round as though looking to escape, then set off full belt, shouting, across the concrete on to the field. Mr Sugden set off after him.

'Casper! Shut up, lad! What are you trying to do, disrupt the whole school?'

He gained on Billy, and as he drew near swiped at him with his flat hand. Billy, watching the blows, zig-zagged out of reach, just ahead of them.

'I'm frozen, Sir! I'm shoutin' to keep warm!'

'Well don't shout at me then! I'm not a mile away!'

They were shouting at each other as though they were aboard ship in a gale. Mr Sugden tried to swat him again. Billy side-stepped, and threw him off balance. So he slowed to a walk and turned round, blowing his whistle and beckoning the others to hurry up.

'Come on, you lot! Hurry up!'

They started to run at speeds ranging from jogging to sprinting, and arrived within a few seconds of each other on the senior football pitch.

'Line up on the halfway line and let's get two sides picked!'

They lined up, jumping and running on the spot, those with long sleeves clutching the cuffs in their hands, those without massaging their goosey arms.

'Tibbut, come out here and be the other captain.'

Tibbut walked out and stood facing the line, away from Mr Sugden.

'I'll have first pick, Tibbut.'

'That's not right, Sir.'

'Why isn't it?'

''Cos you'll get all the best players.'

'Rubbish, lad.'

'Course you will, Sir. It's not fair.'

'Tibbut. Do you want to play football? Or do you want to get dressed and go and do some maths?'

'Play football, Sir.'

'Right then, stop moaning and start picking. I'll have Anderson.'

He turned away from Tibbut and pointed to a boy who was standing on one of the intersections of the centre circle and the halfway line. Anderson walked off this cross and stood behind him. Tibbut scanned the line, considering his choice.

'I'll have Purdey.'

'Come on then, Ellis.'

Each selection altered the structure of the line. When Tibbut had been removed from the centre, all the boys sidestepped to fill the gap. The same happened when Anderson went from near one end. But when Purdey and Ellis, who had been standing side by side, were removed, the boys at their shoulders stood still, therefore dividing the original line into two. These new lines were swiftly segmented as more boys were chosen, leaving no trace of the first major division, just half a dozen boys looking across spaces at each other; reading from left to right: a fat boy; an arm's length away, two friends, one tall with glasses, the other short with a hare-lip; then a space of two yards and Billy; a boy space away from him, a thin boy with a crew-cut and a spotty face; and right away from these, at the far end of the line, another fat boy. Spotty Crew-Cut was halfway between the two fat boys, therefore half of the length of the line was occupied by five of the boys. The far fat boy was the next to go, which halved the length of the line and left Spotty Crew-Cut as one of the end markers.

Tibbut then selected the tall friend with glasses. Mr Sugden immediately selected his partner. They separated gradually as they walked away from the line, parting finally to enter their respective teams. And then there were three: Fatty, Billy, and Spotty Crew-Cut, blushing across at each other while the captains considered. Tibbut picked Crew-Cut. He dashed forward into the anonymity of his team. Fatty stood grinning. Billy stared down at the earth. After long deliberation Mr Sugden chose Billy, leaving Tibbut with Hobson's choice; but before either

Billy or Fatty could move towards their teams, Mr Sugden was already turning away and shouting instructions.

'Right! We'll play down hill!'

The team broke for their appropriate halves, and while they were arguing their claims for positions, Mr Sugden jogged to the sideline, dropped the ball, and took off his tracksuit. Underneath he was wearing a crisp red football shirt with white cuffs and a white band round the neck. A big white 9 filled most of the back, whiter than his white nylon shorts, which showed a slight fleshy tint through the material. He pulled his socks up, straightened the ribs, then took a fresh roll of half inch bandage from his tracksuit and ripped off two lengths. The torn bandage packet, the cup of its structure still intact, blew away over the turf like the damaged shell of a dark blue egg. Mr Sugden used the lengths of bandage to secure his stockings just below the knees, then he folded his tracksuit neatly on the ground, looked down at himself, and walked on to the pitch carrying the ball like a plum pudding on the tray of his hand. Tibbut, standing on the centre circle, with his hands down his shorts, winked at his Left Winger and waited for Mr Sugden to approach.

'Who are you today, Sir, Liverpool?'

'Rubbish, lad! Don't you know your club colours yet?'

'Liverpool are red, aren't they, Sir?'

'Yes, but they're all red, shirts, shorts and stockings. These are Manchester United's colours.'

'Course they are, Sir, I forgot. What position are you playing?'

Mr Sugden turned his back on him to show him the number 9.

'Bobby Charlton. I though you were usually Denis Law when you were Manchester United.'

'It's too cold to play as a striker today. I'm scheming this morning, all over the field like Charlton.'

'Law plays all over, Sir. He's not only a striker.'

'He doesn't link like Charlton.'

'Better player though, Sir.'

Sugden shook his head. 'No, he's been badly off form recently.'

'Makes no odds, he's still a better player. He can settle a game in two minutes.'

'Are you trying to tell *me* about football, Tibbut?'

'No, Sir.'

'Well shut up then. Anyway Law's in the wash this week.'

He placed the ball on the centre spot and looked round at his team. There was only Billy out of position. He was standing between the full backs, the three of them forming a domino : : : pattern with the half backs. The goal was empty. Mr Sugden pointed at it.

'There's no one in goal!'

His team looked round to confirm this observation, but Tibbut's team had beaten them to it by just looking straight ahead.

'Casper! What position are you supposed to be playing?'

Billy looked to the Right Back, the Left Back, the Right Back again. Neither of them supplied the answer, so he answered the question himself.

'I don't know, Sir. Inside Right?'

This answer made 1 : Mr Sugden angry. 2 : the boys laugh.

'Don't talk ridiculous, lad! How can you be playing Inside Right back there?'

He looked up at the sky.

'God help us; fifteen years old and still doesn't know the positions of a football team!'

He levelled one arm at Billy.

'Get in goal lad!'

'O, Sir! I can't goal. I'm no good.'

'Now's your chance to learn then, isn't it?'

'I'm fed up o' goin' in goal. I go in every week.'

Billy turned round and looked at the goal as though it was the portal leading into the gladiatorial arena.

'Don't stand looking lad. Get in there!'

'Well don't blame me then, when I let 'em all through.'

'Of course I'll blame you, lad! Who do you expect me to blame?'

Billy cursed him quietly all the way back to the nets.

Sugden (commentator): 'And both teams are lined up for the

kick off in this vital fifth-round cup-tie, Manchester United versus ...?' Sugden (teacher) : 'Who are we playing, Tibbut?'

'Er ... we'll be Liverpool, Sir.'

'You can't be Liverpool.'

'Why not, Sir?'

'I've told you once, they're too close to Manchester United's colours aren't they?'

Tibbut massaged his brow with his fingertips, and under this guise of thinking, glanced round at his team : Goalkeeper, green polo. Right Back, blue and white stripes. Left Back, green and white quarters. Right Half, white cricket. Centre Half, all blue. Left Half, all yellow. Right Wing, orange and green rugby. Inside Right, black T. Centre Forward, blue denim tab collar. Tibbut, red body white sleeves. Left Wing, all blue.

'We'll be Spurs then, Sir. They'll be no clash of colours then.'

'... And it's Manchester United v. Spurs in this vital fifth-round cup-tie.'

Mr Sugden (referee) sucked his whistle and stared at his watch, waiting for the second finger to twitch back up to twelve. 5 4 3 2. He dropped his wrist and blew. Anderson received the ball from him, sidestepped a tackle from Tibbut then cut it diagonally between two opponents into a space to his left. Sugden (player) running into this space, raised his left foot to trap it, but the ball rolled under his studs. He veered left, caught it, and started to cudgel it upfield in a travesty of a dribble, sending it too far ahead each time he touched it, so that by the time he had progressed twenty yards, he had crash-tackled it back from three Spurs defenders. His left winger, unmarked and lonely out on the touchline, called for the ball, Sugden heard him, looked at him, then kicked the ball hard along the ground towards him. But even though the wingman started to spring as soon as he read its line, it still shot out of play a good ten yards in front of him. He slithered to a stop and whipped round.

'Hey up, Sir! What do you think I am?'

'You should have been moving, lad. You'd have caught it then.'

'What do you think I wa' doin', standing still?'

'It was a perfectly good ball!'

'Ar, for a whippet perhaps!'

'Don't argue with me, lad! And get that ball fetched!'

The ball had rolled and stopped on the roped-off cricket square. The left winger left the pitch and walked towards it. He scissor-jumped the rope, picked the ball up off the lush lawn, then volleyed it straight back on to the pitch without bouncing it once on the intervening stretch of field.

Back in the goal, Billy was giant-striding along the goal line, counting the number of strides from post to post: five and a bit. He turned, propelled himself off the post and jump-strode across to the other side: five. After three more attempts he reduced this record to four and a half, then he returned along the line, heel-toe, heel-toeing it: thirty pump lengths.

After fourteen minutes' play he touched the ball for the first time. Tibbut, dribbling in fast, pushed the ball between Mr Sugden's legs, ran round him and delivered the ball out to his right winger, who took it in his stride, beat his Full Back and centred for Tibbut, who had continued his run, to outjump Mr Sugden and head the ball firmly into the top right-hand corner of the goal. Billy watched it fly in, way up on his left, then he turned round and picked it up from under the netting.

'Come on Casper! Make an effort, lad!'

'I couldn't save that, Sir.'

'You could have tried.'

'What for, Sir, when I knew I couldn't save it?'

'We're playing this game to win you know, lad.'

'I know, Sir.'

'Well, try then!'

He held his hands out to receive the ball. Billy obliged, but as it left his hand the wet leather skidded off his skin and it dropped short in the mud, between them. He ran out to retrieve it, but Sugden had already started towards it, and when Billy saw the stare of his eyes and the set of his jaw as he ran at the ball, he stopped and dropped down, and the ball missed him and went over him, back into the net. He knelt up, his left arm, left side and left leg striped with mud.

'What wa' that for, Sir?'

'Slack work, lad. Slack work.'

He retrieved the ball himself, and carried it quickly back to the centre for the restart. Billy stood up, a mud pack stuck to each knee. He pulled his shirt sleeve round and started to furrow the mud with his finger nails.

'Look at this lot. I've to keep this shirt on an' all after.'

The Right Back was drawn by this lament, but was immediately distracted by a chorus of warning shouts, and when he turned round he saw the ball running loose in his direction. He ran at it head down, and toed it far up field, showing no interest in its flight or destination, but turning to commiserate with Billy almost as soon as it had left his boot. It soared over the halfway line, and Sugden started to chase. It bounced, once, twice, then rolled out towards the touchline. He must catch it, and the rest of his forward line moved up in anticipation of the centre. But the ball, decelerating rapidly as though it wanted to be caught, still crossed the line before he could reach it. His disappointed Forwards muttered amongst themselves as they trooped back out of the penalty area.

'He should have caught that, easy.'

'He's like a chuffing carthorse.'

'Look at him, he's knackered.'

'Hopeless tha means.'

Tibbut picked the ball up for the throw in.

'Hard luck, Sir.'

Sugden, hands on hips, chest heaving, had his Right Back in focus a good thirty seconds before he had sufficient control over his respiration to remonstrate with him.

'Come on, lad! Find a man with this ball! Don't just kick it anywhere!'

The Right Back, his back turned, continued his conversation with Billy.

'S P A R R O W!'

'What, Sir?'

'I'm talking to you, lad!'

'Yes, Sir.'

'Well pay attention then and get a grip of your game. We're losing, lad.'

96

'Yes, Sir.'

Manchester United equalised soon after when the referee awarded them a penalty. Sugden scored.

At the other end of the pitch, Billy was busy with the netting. He was standing with his back to the play, clawing the fibres and growling like a little lion. He stuck a paw through a square and pawed at a visitor, withdrew it and stalked across his cage. The only other exhibit was the herd of multi-coloured cross-breeds gambolling around the ball behind him. The rest of the grounds were deserted. The main body of the collection was housed in the building across the fields, and all round the fields a high wire fence had been constructed. Round the top of the fence strands of barbed wire were affixed to inward-leaning angle-irons. Round the bottom, a ridge of shaggy grass grew where the mower had missed, and underneath the wire the grass had been cut in a severe fringe by the concrete flags of the pavement. The road curved round the field in a crescent, and across the road the row of council houses mirrored this exact curve. Field Crescent.

Billy gripped a post between both hands, inserted one raised foot into a square in the side netting, then, using this as a stirrup, heaved himself up and grabbed hold of the cross-bar. He hand-over-handed it to the middle and rested, swinging loosely backwards and forwards with his legs together. Then he let go with one hand and started to scratch his arm pits, kicking his legs and imitating chimp sounds. The bar shook, and the rattling of the bolts turned several heads, and soon all the boys were watching him, the game forgotten.

'Casper! Casper, get down lad! What do you think you are, an ape?'

'No, Sir, I'm just keeping warm.'

'Well get down then, before I come and make you red hot!'

Billy grasped the bar again with both hands, adjusted his grip, and began to swing : forward and back, forward and back, increasing momentum with thrusts of his legs. Forward and back, upwards and back, legs horizontal as he swung upwards and back. Horizontal and back, horizontal both ways, hands leaving bar at the top of each swing. Forward and back, just one more time; then a rainbow flight down, and a landing knees bent.

He needed no steps or staggering to correct his balance, but stood up straight, smiling; the cross-bar still quivering.

Applause broke out. Sugden silenced it.

'Right, come on then, let's get on with this G A M E.'

The score : still 1–1.

1–2. When Billy, shielding his face, deflected a stinger up on to the cross-bar, and it bounced down behind him and over the line.

2–2. When the referee, despite protests, allowed a goal by Anderson to count, even though he appeared to score it from an offside position.

A dog appeared at the edge of the field, a lean black mongrel, as big as an Alsatian, sniffing around the bottom of the fence on the pavement side. A second later it was inside, bounding across the field to join the game. It skidded round the ball, barking. The boy on the ball got off it, quick. The dog lay on its front legs, back curved, tail up continuing the line of its body. The boys ganged up at a distance, 'yarring' and threatening, but every time one of them moved towards it, the dog ran at him, jumping and barking, scattering the lot of them before turning and running back to the ball.

The boys were as excited as children playing 'Mr Wolf'. Carefully they closed in, then, when one of them made his effort to retrieve the ball, and the dog retaliated, they all scattered, screaming, to form up again twenty yards away and begin a new advance. If Mr Sugden had had a gun, Mr Wolf would have been dead in no time.

'Whose is it? Who does it belong to?' (From the back of the mob as it advanced, leading it when they retreated.) 'Somebody go and fetch some cricket bats from the storeroom, they'll shift it.'

In the excitement nobody took any notice of him, so he looked round and saw Billy, who was stamping patterns in the goalmouth mud.

'Casper!'

'What, Sir?'

'Come here!'

'What, Sir?'

'Go and fetch half a dozen cricket bats from the games store.'

'Cricket bats, Sir! What, in this weather?'

'No you fool! To shift that dog – it's ruining the game.'

'You don't need cricket bats to do that, Sir.'

'What do you need then, dynamite?'

'It'll not hurt you.'

'I'm not giving it a chance. I'd sooner take meat away from a starving lion than take the ball away from that thing.'

The dog was playing with the ball, holding it between its front paws, and with its head on one side, trying to bite it. However its jaws were too narrow, and each time it closed them its teeth pushed the ball forward out of reach. Then it shuffled after it, growling and rumbling in its throat. Billy walked forward, patting one thigh and clicking his tongue on the roof of his mouth. The other boys got down to their marks.

'Come on then, lad. Come on.'

It came. Bouncing up to his chest and down and round him. He reached out and scuffled its head each time it bounced up to his hand.

'What's up wi'thi? What's up then, you big daft sod?'

It rested its front paws on his chest and barked bright-eyed into his face, its tongue turning up at the edges and slithering in and out as it breathed. Billy fondled its ears, then walked away from it, making it drop down on all fours.

'Come on then, lad. Come on. Where do you want me to take him, Sir?'

'Anywhere, lad. Anywhere as long as you get it off this field.'

'Do you want me to find out where it lives, Sir, and take it home? I can be dressed in two ticks.'

'No. No, just get it off the field and get back in your goal.'

Billy hooked his finger under the dog's collar and led it firmly towards the school, talking quietly to it all the time.

When he returned they were leading 3–2.

A few minutes later they were level 3–3.

'What's the matter, Casper, are you scared of the ball?'

Mr Sugden studied his watch, as the ball was returned to him at the centre spot.

'Right then, the next goal's the winner!'

One to make and the match to win.

End to end play. Excitement. Thrills. OOOO! Arrr! Goal! No! It was over the line, Sir! Play on!

Billy snatched the ball up, ran forward, and volleyed it up the field. He turned round and hopped back, pulling a sucked lemon face.

'Bloody hell, it's like lead, that ball. It's just like gettin' t'stick across your feet.'

He stood stork fashion and manipulated his foot. Every time he turned his toes up water squeezed into the folds of the instep of his pump.

'Bugger me. I'm not kicking that again.'

He placed the foot lightly to the ground and tested his weight on it.

'I feel champion, bones broke in one foot, frostbite in t'other.'

He unrolled his shorts up to his neck and pushed his arms down inside them.

'Come on, Sugden, blow that bloody whistle, I'm frozen.'

The game continued. Sugden shot over the bar. Seconds later he prevented Tibbut from shooting by tugging his shirt. Penalty! Play on.

Billy sighted the school behind one outstretched thumb and obliterated it by drawing the thumb slowly to his eye. A young midget walked from behind the nail. Billy opened his other eye and dropped his hand. More midgets were leaving the midget building, walking down the midget drive to the midget gates. Billy ran out to the edge of the penalty area, his arms back at attention down his shorts.

'Bell's gone, Sir! They're comin' out!'

'Never mind the bell, get back in your goal!'

'I'm on first sitting, Sir. I'll miss my dinner.'

'I thought I told you to swap sittings when you had games.'

'I forgot, Sir.'

'Well you'd better forget about your dinner then.'

He turned back to the game, then did a double take.

'And get your arms out of your shorts, lad! You look as if you've had Thalidomide!'

Play developed at the other end. Billy stayed on the edge of the penalty area, forming a trio with his Full Backs.

'How can I stop to second dinners when I've to go home an' feed my hawk?'

All the toys had disappeared from the playground, some of them growing into boys as they walked up Field Crescent and passed level with the pitch. They shouted encouragement through the wire, then shrank and disappeared round the curve. They were replaced by a man and a woman approaching in the same direction, on opposite pavements. The man was wearing a grey suit, the woman a green coat, and as they drew level with the field they merged on to the same plane, and were suddenly pursued by a red car. Three blocks of colour, red, grey and green, travelling on the same plane, in the same direction, and at different speeds. Stop. Red, grey and green. Above the green of the field, against the red of the houses, and below the grey of the sky. Start. The car wove between the two pedestrians, drawing its noise between them like a steel hawser. A few seconds later the man passed the woman, grey-green merging momentarily, and seconds later the woman opened a garden gate and disappeared from the scene, leaving the man isolated on the Crescent. Silence. Then the burst of a motor bike, Rrm! Rrm! revving behind the houses, fading, to allow a thunk of the ball. A call, an echo, an empty yard. A sheet of paper captured against the wire by the wind.

12.15 p.m. The winning goal suddenly became important, no more laughter, no more joking, everybody working. For most of the game most of the boys had been as fixed as buttons on a pinball machine, sparking into life only when the nucleus of footballers amongst them had occasionally shuttled the ball into their defined areas : mere props to the play. Now they were all playing. Both teams playing as units, and positions were taken seriously. In possession they moved and called for the ball from spaces. Out of possession they marked and tackled hard to win it back. A move provoked a counter move, which in turn determined moves made by players in other segments of the pitch. The ball was a magnet, exerting the strongest pull on the players nearest to it, and still strong enough to activate the players farthest away.

12.20 p.m. Billy jump, jump, jumped on the line. 'Score, for Christ's sake somebody score.' Tick tick tick tick. Sugden missed again. He's blind, he's bleedin' blind. Sugden was crimson and sweating like a drayhorse, and boys began to accelerate smoothly past him, well wide of him, well clear of his scything legs and shirt-grabbing fists.

Manchester United came under serious pressure. Sugden retreated to his own penalty area, tackling and clearing and hoping for a breakaway. But back it came, back they came, all Tibbut's team except the goalkeeper advancing into Sugden's half, making the pitch look as unbalanced as the 6 : 1 domino.

But still Sugden held them, held them by threatening his own players into desperate heriocs. But it had to come. It must.

12.25 p.m. 26. 27. Every time Billy saved a shot he looked heartbroken. Every time he cleared the ball, he cleared it blind, giving the other side a fifty-fifty chance of possession, and every time they gained possession, Sugden threatened him with violence, while at the same time keeping his eyes on the ball and moving out to check the next advance. So that a sudden spectator would have been surprised to see Sugden rushing forward and apparently intimidating the boy on the ball.

For one shot, coming straight to him, Billy dived, but the ball hit his legs and ricocheted round the post. Corner! Well saved, Casper. No joke. No laughter.

It was a good corner, the ball dropping close to the penalty spot. A shot – blocked, a tackle, a scramble, falling, fouling, W H O O S H, Sugden shifted it out. 'O U T. Get out! Get up that field!'

Billy scraped a lump of mud up and unconsciously began to mould it in his fist, elongating it to a sausage, then rolling it to a dumpling, picking pellets from it and flicking them with his thumb, until nothing remained but a few drying flakes on his crusty palm. He scraped another lump up and began again; rolling, moulding, flicking, then he pivoted and wanged it across the goal at the posts. FLOP. It stuck, and when the next shot came towards him he dived flamboyantly and made an elaborate pretence to save it, but the ball bounced over his arms and rolled slowly into the net.

GOAL!

Tibbut's team immediately abandoned the pitch and raced across the field, arms flying, cheering. Billy raced after them without even bothering to pick the ball out of the net, or look at his own team, or at Mr Sugden.

He was slipping his jacket on when Sugden entered the changing room. Sugden watched him, then, as Billy headed for the door he stepped across and blocked his path.

'In a hurry, Casper?'

'Yes, Sir, I've to get home.'

'Really?'

'Yes, Sir.'

'Haven't you forgotten something?'

Billy looked back at the bare peg and the space beneath it.

'No, Sir.'

'Are you sure?'

Billy inspected himself, then looked up into Sugden's face.

'Yes, Sir.'

Sugden smiled at him. Stalemate. Billy looked past him, and by transferring his weight from foot to foot was able to see the door, one eyed, round each side of him. Right eye, left eye. Right eye, left.

'What about the showers?'

He nodded over Billy's head towards the steam clouding above the partition wall at the far end of the room. Billy stopped rocking.

'I've had one, Sir.'

Sugden back-handed him hard across the cheek, swinging his face, and knocking him back into an avenue of clothing.

'Liar!'

'I have Sir! I was first through! Ask anybody.'

He stroked his cheek, his eyes brimming.

'Right, I will.'

Sugden whipped his whistle out of his tracksuit bottoms and blew a long shrill blast, which was still echoing long after the boys had come to order, and for a few seconds produced a ringing silence of its own which was audible even above the hiss of the showers, and the gurgle at the grate.

'Put your hands up if you saw Casper have a shower.'

No hands. No replies. The boys continued their activities quietly. Some were dressing, tousle-haired. Some were drying themselves on the terrace of stone tiles set before the showers. The rest, who had crowded to both ends of the partition wall, drifted back behind it and continued their shower. One boy posed Eros-like, and allowed a jet of water to play into his palm and waterfall out on to the tiles of the drying area. Most of these tiles were varnished with water. their slippery surfaces a-jiggle with the movements of the boys and the refractions from the strip lights in the ceiling. Under the walls a few tiles remained dry, their grey matt surfaces insensitive to this movement and light.

'Well Casper, I thought anybody would tell me?' Pause. 'Purdey, did you see him under the showers?'

'No, Sir.'

'Ellis?'

'I didn't see him, Sir.'

'Tibbut?'

He shook his head without even bothering to look up from drying between his toes.

'Do you want me to ask anybody else, Casper? – You lying rat!'

'My mam says I haven't to have a shower, Sir. I've got a cold.'

'Let's see your note then.'

Smiling, he held his hand out. Billy produced nothing to place in it.

'I haven't got one, Sir.'

'Well get undressed then.'

'I can bring one this afternoon though.'

'That's no good lad, I want one now. You know the school rule, don't you? Any boy wishing to be excused Physical

104

Education or showers must, AT THE TIME of the lesson, produce a sealed letter of explanation signed by one of his parents or legal guardian.'

'Oh, go on, Sir, I've to get home.'

'You can get home, Casper.'

'Can I, Sir?'

His face brightened and he started to move round Sugden towards the door. Sugden performed a little chassé, and reproduced their former positions.

'As soon as you've had a shower.'

'I've no towel, Sir.'

'Borrow one.'

'Nobody'll lend me one.'

'Well you'll have to drip-dry then, won't you?'

He thought this was funny. Billy didn't. So Sugden looked round for a more appreciative audience. But no one was listening. They faced up for a few more seconds, then Billy turned back to his peg. He undressed quickly, bending his pumps free of his heels and sliding them off without untying the laces. When he stood up the black soles of his socks stamped damp imprints on the dry floor, which developed into a haphazard set of footprints when he removed his socks and stepped around pulling his jeans down. His ankles and heels were ingrained with ancient dirt which seemed to belong to the pigmentation of his skin. His left leg sported a mud stripe, and both his knees were encrusted. The surfaces of these mobile crusts were hair-lined, and with every flexion of the knee these lines opened into frown-like furrows.

For an instant, as he hurried into the showers, with one leg angled in running, with his dirty legs and huge rib cage moulding the skin of his white body, with his hollow cheek in profile, and the sabre of shadow emanating from the eye-hole, just for a moment he resembled an old print of a child hurrying towards the final solution.

The hot water made him gasp as though it was cold. He stood on tiptoes and raised his arms against it, the hairs on his forearms pulling the skin up to goose pimples.

The nozzles, sprouting from parallel pipes, were arranged in a zig-zag pattern so that each one sprouted into the space between two nozzles on the opposite wall. Billy backed into the corner, his arms pressed at right angles against the adjoining walls, trying to outdistance the range of the end nozzle. Then, after a glance to map his driest route, he darted through, ducking and skidding, bouncing from wall to wall, creeping under the walls, looking up at the nozzles and twisting away from their flow into the next one, out of it, under it, through it, his feet slicing the sheet of ground water into bow waves as he crashed through to the other end. Sugden was waiting for him as he turned the corner to come out.

'In a hurry, Casper?'

He closed the gap with his body as Billy tried to squeeze past him.

'What's the rush, lad?'

'Can I come out, Sir?'

He considered, while the end nozzle was playing on Billy's back and the back of his head.

'You're not going anywhere 'til you've got all that mud off and had a proper wash.'

Billy turned back into the showers and began to scour himself with his hands. The mud on his legs had blackened, and was being eroded by the incessant raining and streaming down his thighs. Rivulets of mud coursed from his knees, down the ridges of the tibia to the tiles, to be swept away and replenished with a gush as Billy swept his hands over his knees, and the mud stained his shins, and the tiles, to be swept away, to the gutter, to the grate.

While he worked on his ankles and heels Sugden stationed three boys at one end of the showers and moved to the other end, where the controls fed into the pipes on the wall. The wheel controlling the issue was set on a short stem, and divided into eight petal-shaped segments. A thermometer was fixed to the junction of the hot and cold water pipes, its dial sliced red up to 109 F., and directly below the thermometer was a chrome lever on a round chrome base, stamped HOT. WARM. COLD. The blunt arrow was pointing to HOT. Sugden swung it back over WARM TO COLD. For a few seconds there was no visible change in the temperature, and the red slice held steady, still dominating the dial. Then it began to recede, slowly at first, then swiftly, its share of the face diminishing rapidly.

The cold water made Billy gasp. He held out his hands as though testing for rain, then ran for the end. The three guards barred the exit.

'Hey up, shift! Let me out, you rotten dogs!'

They held him easily so he swished back to the other end, yelling all the way along. Sugden pushed him in the chest as he clung his way round the corner.

'Got a sweat on, Casper?'

'Let me out, Sir. Let me come.'

'I thought you'd like a cooler after your exertions in goal.'

'I'm frozen!'

'Really?'

'Gi' o'er, Sir! It's not right!'

'And was it right when you let the last goal in?'

'I couldn't help it!'

'Rubbish, lad.'

Billy tried another rush. Sugden repelled it, so he tried the other end again. Every time he tried to escape the three boys bounced him back, stinging him with their snapping towels as he retreated. He tried manoeuvring the nozzles, but whichever way he twisted them the water still found him out. Until finally he gave up, and stood amongst them, tolerating the freezing spray in silence.

When Billy stopped yelling the other boys stopped laughing, and when time passed and no more was heard from him, their conversations began to peter out, and attention gradually focused on the showers. Until only a trio was left shouting into each other's faces, unaware that the volume of noise in the room had dropped. Suddenly they stopped, looked round embarrassed, then looked towards the showers with the rest of the boys.

The cold water had cooled the air, the steam had vanished, and the only sound that came from the showers was the beat of water behind the partition; a mesmeric beat which slowly drew the boys together on the drying area.

The boy guards began to look uneasy, and they looked across to their captain.

'Can we let him out now, Sir?'

'No!'

'He'll get pneumonia.'

'I don't care what he gets, I'll show him! If he thinks I'm running my blood to water for ninety minutes, and then having the game deliberately thrown away at the last minute, he's another think coming!'

There were signs of unrest and much muttering amongst the crowd:

'He's had enough, Sir.'

'It was only a game.'

'Let him go.'

'Shut up, you lot, and get out!'

Nobody moved. They continued to stare at the partition wall as though a film was being projected on to its tiled surface.

Then Billy appeared over the top of it, hands, head and shoulders, climbing rapidly. A great roar arose, as though Punch had appeared above them hugging his giant cosh. Sugden saw him.

'Get down, Casper!'

Billy straddled the wall and got down, on the dry side. There was laughing – (and gnashing of teeth). The three guards deserted their posts. Sugden turned the showers off, and the crowd dispersed. Billy planed the standing droplets off his body and limbs with his palms, then hurried to his peg and dabbed himself with his shorts. His shirt stuck and ruttled down his back when he pulled it on, and the damp seeped through the light grey flannel, staining it charcoal.

＊

Home, straight home, and straight down the garden to the shed. He looked between the bars, clicking his tongue. The hawk lobbed off her perch, and with one wing-flick reached the shelf behind the door. Billy tapped the bars, then hurried back up the path to the garage.

Inside, on a bench built across the back, was a round board with B R E A D carved in relief round its perimeter. The wood was scrubbed white, and hundreds of knife cuts had criss-crossed the surface into tiny geometrical figures. Across the board lay a knife, its blade gleaming stainless, in contrast to the ground steel of its teeth. Two brass rivets secured the handle, which was as smooth and dead as driftwood. Beside the board lay a leather satchel, and a scrubbing brush, bristles up.

Billy lifted the flap of the satchel and took out a grease-proof paper packet. When he opened it a few pieces of beef were stuck to the paper like Elastoplast. He sniff-sniffed the beef, then placed in on the board and went outside.

He crossed to the kitchen door, unlocked it, and walked straight through the kitchen to the living-room. It was cold and quiet, and darkness shaded the corners. Articles of clothing littered the furniture, their shapes determined by the weight and textures of the materials; woollen clumps, cotton spreads and a nylon slip slithering over one arm of the settee. On the table used crockery was grouped about the checked cloth like the pieces of an abandoned game. Billy knelt down and felt under the settee. He came up with an air rifle, then crossed to the fireplace and reached up to a Toby Jug, looking pleased with himself at one end of the mantelpiece. He was full of lead pellets. Billy tipped him up and a soft stream of lead poured out of the black hat into his palm. Then, as he was replacing the jug, he noticed the two half-crowns holding down a folded slip of paper next to the clock. The coins fitted perfectly, their bevelled edges corresponding to form one thick crown. He paused, his fingers still round the jug. Then he turned and walked away, stopped, and looked back at the mantelpiece. He broke the rifle open and fitted a slug, frowning and nibbling his bottom lip, and patting at the slug with his thumb long after it had snugged into position. A smear of grease stained the end of his thumb. He studied it, then lubricated the tip of his forefinger by rubbing finger and thumb together.

The gun was .22 calibre, fitted with telescopic sights.

'Right then, odds I take it, evens I don't.'

He raised the rifle and aimed at the clock, the hairlines of the sights dividing the face like a hot-cross bun. He panned across to the Toby Jug, sighting the grin, the belly, the beer mug, then brought it back across to the money and squeezed the trigger. The top coin spun up as though tossed by a thumb, reaching its zenith as the bottom one bounced out of the hearth on to the rug, heads, while the top one rattled and settled on the mantel-piece Re Re Re Re Rrrrrrrrrr, tails, and the betting slip zig-zagged in ever increasing arcs out under the table. Billy ran across to discover his luck.

'Shit!'

He dropped the coins into his jacket pocket and crouched under the table for the betting slip. As he stood up he unfolded it.

> 5/-DOUBLE.
> CRACKPOT
> TELL HIM HE'S DEAD.

> ———

> 5/-   J.H.

He refolded the slip and stuffed it into the same pocket as the money, then left the house and shut the door behind him. The noise made a starling fly off the gutter, making Billy glance up as he locked the door.

He entered the garage, opened the back window, the side window, then placed a stool over a chalk X, drawn in a posi-tion where he could see squarely through both windows by merely turning his head. He settled down on the stool to wait. Nothing happened. He sat with the rifle across his thighs, whistl-ing softly and rocking his feet silently in tune. He stopped whistling and rocking when a house sparrow landed on top of the kestrel's hut. He crept to the back window. When he raised his head the sparrow had gone. So he crept back to his stool and settled again.

There was a continuous CHIP CHIP of sparrows, but the only ones in view were out of range specks on chimney turrets. Then a cock sparrow landed on the gutter above the back bed-room window. It stood on one leg and scratched its beak with a high speed shuttering of the other foot, roused its feathers and settled, its fluffed body curving up over the gutter like an egg in a cup. Billy slipped off his stool to the window and eased one eye round the frame. Still there. He lifted the rifle and slowly poked it out, angling and swivelling it in the sparrow's direction. The sparrow stopped chipping and looked about, its feathers slicking to its body, revealing its true thin shape. Billy froze. Pause. The sparrow relaxed, and continued its song, chip. chip. chip. Billy scroamed into a comfortable kneeling position, and, jacking his left elbow on the window ledge and steadying the barrel on the side of the frame, brought the sparrow into sight. A grey pom-pom with a black bib; a grey capped head turning in profile to silhouette the tiny beak splitting wide at each utterance. A well defined study, edged black against the slate background. Billy adjusted the sights just a shade to pinpoint the intersection of the hairlines on to the bib. Hold it. Squeeeeze. The kick back made him jump and blink and open both eyes in time to see the sparrow plumping head first wings out down the back-cloth of brick. Reloading the rifle he ran out to where the sparrow lay on the concrete. He touched it with the barrel tip, then carefully turned it over. It lay still. So he bent down and picked it up. Both eyes were closed. A thin line of blood emphasised the division of the beak, but there was no further sign of violence. Billy scuffed the plumage on its breast, and fanned its wings to look underneath them. But there was no mark where the slug had entered. He smoothed the feathers and refolded the wings, then held the rifle out at arms length and fired it down into the soil near his feet. No earth flew, and there was no sign where the pellet had entered. Just the same still formation of sods and pocked earth.

He took the sparrow back into the garage, put it into the satchel, and took out the lure. He tied a scrap of beef to each side of it, then replaced it and checked the contents of the satchel; front pocket – penknife, whistle, creance; back pocket – swivel and leash, lure, sparrow – and beef scraps. He put the satchel on, took his gauntlet down from a nail above the bench and left the garage.

The hawk was waiting for him. As he unlocked the door she screamed and pressed her face to the bars. He selected the largest piece of beef, then, holding it firmly between finger and thumb with most of it concealed in his palm, he eased the door open and shoved his glove through the space. The hawk jumped on to his glove and attacked the meat. Billy swiftly followed his fist into the hut, secured the door behind him, and while the hawk was tearing at the fringe of beef, he attached her swivel and leash.

As soon as they got outside she looked up and tensed, feathers flat, eyes threatening. Billy stood still, whistling softly, waiting for her to relax and resume her feeding. Then he walked round the back of the hut and held her high over his head as he climbed carefully over the fence. A tall hawthorn hedge bordered one side of the field, and the wind was strong and constant in the branches, but in the field it had been strained to a whisper. He reached the centre and unwound the leash from his glove, pulled it free of the swivel, then removed the swivel from the jesses and raised his fist. The hawk flapped her wings and fanned her tail, her claws still gripping the glove. Billy cast her off by nudging his glove upwards, and she banked away, completed a wide circuit then gained height rapidly, while he took the lure from his bag and unwound the line from the stick.

'Come on, Kes! Come on then!'

He whistled and swung the lure short-lined on a vertical plane. The hawk turned, saw it, and stooped. . . .

'Casper!'

He glanced involuntarily across the field. Mr Farthing was climbing the fence and waving to him. The hawk grabbed the lure and Billy allowed her to take it to the ground.

'Bloody hell fire.'

He pegged the stick into the soil and stood up. Mr Farthing was tiptoeing towards him, concentrating on his passage through the grass. With his overcoat on, and his trousers pinched up, he looked like a day-tripper paddling at the seaside. Billy allowed him to get within thirty yards, then stopped him by raising one hand.

'You'll have to stop there, Sir.'

'I hope I'm not too late.'

'No, Sir, but you'll have to watch from there.'

'That's all right. If you think I'm too near I can go back to the fence.'

'No, you'll be all right there, as long as you stand still.'

'I won't breathe.'

He smiled and put his hands in his overcoat pockets. Billy crouched down and made in towards the hawk along the lure line. He offered her a scrap of beef, and she stepped off the lure on to his glove. He allowed her to take the beef, then he stood up and cast her off again. She wheeled away, high round the field. Billy plucked the stick from the ground and began to swing the lure. The hawk turned and stooped at it. Billy watched her as she descended, waiting for the right moment as she accelerated rapidly towards him. Now. He straightened his arm and lengthened the line, throwing the lure into her path and sweeping it before her in a downward arc, then twitching it up too steep for her attack, making her throw up, her impetus carrying her high into the air. She turned and stooped again. Billy presented the lure again. And again. Each time smoothly before her, an inch before her so that the next wing-beat must catch it, or the next. Working the lure like a top matador his cape. Encouraging the hawk, making her stoop faster and harder, making Mr Farthing hold his breath at each stoop and near miss. Each time she made off Billy called her continually, then stopped in concentration as he timed his throw and leaned into the long drawing of the lure and the hawk in its wake, her eyes fixed, beak open, angling her body and adjusting her flight to any slight shift in speed or direction.

She tried a new tactic, and came in low, seeming to flit within a pocket of silence close to the ground. Billy flexed at the knees and flattened the plane of the swing, allowing the lengthening line to pay out before her.

'Come on, this time, Kes! This time!'

She shortened her stoop, and counter stoop, which increased the frequency of her attacks, and made Billy pivot, and whirl, and watch, but never lose control of the lure or its pursuer. Until finally the hawk sheered away and began to ring up high over the hawthorn hedge.

'Come on then, Kes! Once more! Last time!'

And she came, head first, wings closed, swooping down, hurtling down towards Billy, who waited, then lured her — W H O O S H — up, throwing up, ringing up, turning; and as she stooped again Billy twirled the lure and threw it high into her path. She caught it, and clutched it down to the ground.

He allowed her to take the remaining beef scrap from the lure, then took her up and attached the swivel and leash. She looked up sharply at a series of claps. Mr Farthing was applauding softly. Billy started towards him and they met half-way, the hawk fixing the stranger every second of their approach.

'Marvellous, Casper! Brilliant! That's one of the most exciting things I've ever seen!'

Billy blushed, and there was silence while they both looked at the hawk. The hawk looked back, her breast still heaving from her exertions.

'It's beautiful, isn't it? Do you know, this is the first time I've ever been really close to a hawk?'

He raised a hand towards it. The hawk pecked and clawed at it. He withdrew his hand quickly.

'Goodness! ... It's not very friendly, is it?'

Billy smiled and stroked her breast, ruttling under her wings with his fingers.

'Seems all right with you though.'

'Only 'cos she thinks I'm not bothered.'

'What do you mean?'

'Well when she used to peck me I kept my finger there as though it didn't hurt. So after a bit she just packed it in.'

'That's good. I'd never have thought of that.'

'You'll notice I always keep my hands away from her claws though. You don't get used to them striking you.'

Mr Farthing looked at the yellow scaled shins, the four spanned toes, the steely claws gripping the gauntlet.

'No, I'll bet you don't.'

Billy produced the sparrow from his bag and pushed it up between the finger and thumb of his glove. The hawk immediately pinned it with one foot and with her beak began to pluck the feathers from its head. Plucking and tossing in bunches, left and right, sowing them to the wind. Baring a spot, then a patch of puckered pink skin. She nipped this skin and pulled, ripping a hole in it and revealing the pale shine of the skull, as fragile and delicately curved as one of the sparrow's own eggs. Scrunch. The shell crumpled, and the whole crown was torn away and swallowed at one gulp. Another bite and the head was gone; even the beak was swallowed, being first finely crushed into fragments. Billy eased the sparrow up between his fingers, revealing most of its body. The hawk lowered her head and began to pluck the breast and wings. The breast fluff puffed away like fairy clocks; the wing quills twirled to the ground like ash keys. Occasionally the hawk shook her head, trying to dislodge feathers which had stuck to the blood on her beak. If this failed she scratched at them with her claws, the flickering points passing within fractions of her eyes, wincing as though half in enjoyment, half in pain, like someone having a good scratch at a nettle rash.

She cleared most of the breast, then pierced the skin with her beak and tore it open, exposing beneath the wafer of breast meat the minute organs, coiled and compact, packed perfectly into the tiny frame. The hawk disturbed their composition by reaching inside and dragging the intestines out. They swung from her beak, with the stomach attached like a watch on a chain. Then she snuffled and gobbled them down in a slithering putty-coloured pile.

'Uh!'

'Full o' vitamins them, Sir.'

The liver, a purply-brown pad; the heart, a slippery pebble; leaving only the carcass, a mess of skin and bone and feathers, which the hawk pulled apart and devoured in pieces. Any bones which were too big to crush and swallow comfortably were flicked away; clean white fragments, precise miniatures, knobbled and hollowed and lost in the grass. Until only the legs remained. The hawk nibbled delicately at the thighs, stripping them of their last shred of meat, leaving only the tarsi and the feet, which she spat aside. All gone. She stood up and shook her head.

Mr Farthing followed Billy over the fence, round to the front of the shed, and watched through the bars while the hawk was being released inside. She flew straight to her perch, lowered her head and began to feake, using the wood as a strop for her beak. Then she stood up and roused herself. Billy opened the door and stepped aside for Mr Farthing to enter. He squeezed quickly inside and they stood side by side looking at the hawk, which had settled down on one foot, her other foot bunched up in her feathers.

'Keep lookin' away from her, Sir, they don't like being stared at, hawks.'

'Right.'

Mr Farthing glanced round at the whitewashed walls and ceiling, the fresh mutes on the clean shelves, the clean dry sand on the floor.

'You keep it nice and clean in here.'

'You have to. There's less chance of her gettin' sick then.'

'You think a lot about that bird, don't you?'

Billy looked up at him, all the way up to his eyes.

'Course I do. Wouldn't you if it wa' yours?'

Mr Farthing laughed quietly, once.

'Yes I suppose I would. You like wild life, don't you, Billy?'

'Yes, Sir.'

'Have you ever kept any more birds before this one?'

'Stacks. Animals an' all. I had a young fox cub once, reared it an' let it go. It wa' a little blinder.'

'What birds have you kept?'

'All sorts, maggies, jackdaws; I had a young jay once; that wa' murder though, they're right hard to feed, an' it nearly died. I wouldn't have one again, they're best left to their mothers.'

'And which has been your favourite?'

Billy looked at Mr Farthing as though his mentality had suddenly deteriorated to that of an idiot.

'You what, Sir?'

'You mean the hawk?'

'T'others weren't in t'same street.'

'Why not? What's so special about this one?'

Billy bent down and scooped up a fistful of sand.

'I don't know right. It just is that's all.'

'What about magpies? They're handsome birds. And jays, they've got beautiful colours.'

'It's not only t'colours though, that's nowt.'

'What is it then?'

Billy allowed a trickle of sand out of his fist on to his left pump. The grains bounced off the rubber toe cap like a column of tap water exploding in the sink. He shook his head and shrugged his shoulder. Mr Farthing stepped forward and raised one hand.

'What I like about it is its shape; it's so beautifully proportioned. The neat head, the way the wings fold over on its back. Its tail, just the right length, and that down on the thighs, just like a pair of plus-fours.'

He modelled the hawk in the air, emphasising each point of description with corresponding sweeps and curves of his hands.

'It's the sort of thing you want to paint, or model in clay. Painting would be best I should think, you'd be able to get all those lovely brown markings in then.'

'It's when it's flying though, Sir, that's when it's got it over other birds, that's when it's at its best.'

'Yes I agree with you. Do you know, you can tell it's a good flyer just by looking at it sitting there.'

'It's 'cos it looks streamlined.'

'It's what I was saying about proportion, I think that's got something to do with it. There's a saying about racehorses that if they look good, they probably are good. I think the same applies here.'

'It does.'

'And yet there's something weird about it when it's flying.'

'You what, Sir? Hawks are t'best flyers there are.'

'I don't mean ...'

'I'm not sayin' there isn't other good uns; look at swallows and swifts, an' peewits when they're tumblin' about in t'air. An' there's gulls an' all. I used to watch 'em for hours when we used to go away. It wa' t'best at Scarborough, where you could get on t'cliff top an' watch 'em. They're still not t'same though. Not to me anyroad.'

'I don't mean anything to do with the beauty of its flight, that's marvellous. I mean ... well, when it flies there's something about it that makes you feel strange.'

'I think I know what you mean, Sir, you mean everything seems to go dead quiet.'

'That's it!'

His exclamation made the hawk jerk up and tense.

'Steady on, Sir, you'll frighten her to death.'

Mr Farthing pointed two fingers at his temple and triggered his thumb.

'Sorry, I forgot.'

The hawk roused and settled again.

'It was just that you got it so right about the silence.'

'Other folks have noticed that an' all. I know a farmer, an' he says it's the same wi' owls. He says that he's seen 'em catchin' mice in his yard at night, an' that when they swoop down, you feel like poking your ears to make 'em pop because it goes that quiet.'

'Yes, that's right. That's how I felt, it's as though it was flying in a, ... in a, ... in a pocket of silence, that's it, a pocket of silence. That's strange, isn't it?'

'They're strange birds.'

'And this feeling, this silence, it must carry over. Have you noticed how quietly we're speaking? And how strange it sounded when I raised my voice. It was almost like shouting in a church.'

'It's 'cos they're nervous, Sir. You have to keep your voice down.'

'No, it's more than that. It's instinctive. It's a kind of respect.'

'I know, Sir. That's why it makes me mad when I take her out and I'll hear somebody say, "Look there's Billy Casper there wi' his pet hawk." I could shout at 'em; it's not a pet, Sir, hawks are not pets. Or when folks stop me and say, "Is it tame?" Is it heck tame, it's trained that's all. It's fierce, an' it's wild, an' it's not bothered about anybody, not even about me right. And that's why it's great.'

'A lot of people wouldn't understand that sentiment though, they like pets they can make friends with; make a fuss of, cuddle a bit, boss a bit; don't you agree?'

'Ye', I suppose so. I'm not bothered about that though. I'd sooner have her, just to look at her, an' fly her. That's enough for me. They can keep their rabbits an' their cats an' their talkin' budgies, they're rubbish compared wi' her.'

Mr Farthing glanced down at Billy, who was staring at the hawk, breathing rapidly.

'Yes, I think you're right; they probably are.'

'Do you know, Sir, I feel as though she's doin' me a favour just lettin' me stand here.'

'Yes I know what you mean. It's funny though, when you try to analyse it, exactly what it is about it. For example, it's not its size is it?'

'No, Sir.'

'And it doesn't look terribly fearsome; in fact there are moments when it looks positively babyish. So what is it then?'

'I don't know.'

Mr Farthing moulded a fender of sand with the toe of one shoe, then slowly looked up at the hawk.

'I think it's a kind of pride, and as you say independence. It's like an awareness, a satisfaction with its own beauty and prowess. It seems to look you straight in the eye and say, "Who the hell are you anyway?" It reminds me of that poem by Lawrence, "If men were as much men as lizards are lizards they'd be worth looking at." It just seems proud to be itself.'

'Yes, Sir.'

They stood silent for a minute, then Mr Farthing pushed his overcoat and jacket sleeves up to look at the time. The watch face was concealed under his shirt cuff. He revealed the face by lifting the cuff and sliding the strap down his wrist.

'Good lord! Look at the time, it's twenty past one. We'd better be off.'

He fumbled for the door fastener and backed out of the shed.

'I'll give you a lift if you like. I'm in the car.'

Billy blushed and shook his head. Mr Farthing smiled in at him through the bars.

'What's the matter, wouldn't it do your reputation any good to be seen travelling with a teacher?'

'It's not that, Sir. . . . I've one or two things to do first.'

'Please yourself then. But you're going to have to look sharp, or you'll be late.'

'I know. I'll not be long.'

'Right. I'll be off then.'

His face disappeared from the bars, and reappeared a few seconds later.

'And thanks for the display, I really enjoyed it. You're an expert, lad.'

His face disappeared again, and for a few moments his barred charcoal back blocked the whole square. Then light, and other shapes like jigsaw pieces, grew round his receding silhouette, the house, the garage, the garden.

A car engine bleated. Bleated again and caught. BRUM-BRUMMED to a climax, then hummed away on a rising pitch.

Billy looked down and began to guide an oblong furry pellet through the sand with one toe. There was a kink in the fading car sound, a pause like a missed heartbeat as it changed up to a softer tone, and the final fade.

Billy picked the pellet up and inspected it in his palm. It was the size of a blackbird's egg, charcoal coloured, and shining faintly as though lacquered. He rolled it around his hand awhile, sniffed it, then carefully crumbled it with his finger tips. Inside the lacquered crust the fur was a lighter shade of grey, snuff dry, and wrapped inside the fur were tiny bones, and a tiny skull, with sets of dot-size teeth dotted to its tiny jaws. Billy rubbed the fur to ash, and gently blew it away like chaff from grain, leaving only the bones and the skull in his palm. He placed the skull on the shelf behind the door, then began to push the bones around with his forefinger; aimlessly at first, then linking them into a triangle, which he immediately destroyed, and reformed as an angular C. He studied this letter, then tried to remould it, but he could only make a D, so he shuffled the bones until their formation was meaningless.

Selecting the longest bone, he pincered it, pin thin, between his forefinger and thumb. The pressure drained two small patches of his skin white; then the points punctured, and a spot of blood formed on his finger tip; followed by a second on his thumb. He frowned and squeezed. This made him close one eye and bite his lips. The bone remained intact. Billy opened the pincers, and it stuck up out of the skin of his thumb like a little standard. He turned his thumb over, nail upwards. The bone still stuck, so he pulled it out and snapped it. The crack made the hawk open its eyes. Billy dropped the bones and carefully ground them into the sand with his pumps. Only the skull remained. He turned it to face the bars, then quietly left the hut, locked up, and with a final glance at the hawk, walked away up the path.

The betting shop was situated on a square of waste ground between two blocks of houses. At the back, the waste ground was separated from the back gardens of the houses in the next street by a wire fence. At each house a hole had been pulled in this fence, and short cuts led across the waste ground to the pavement.

At various times a path from the door of the betting shop had been contemplated, but never completed. Starting at the door, a double row of housebricks had been set lengthways into the soil, ten bricks long leading into a strip of ashes, which in turn petered out to a final stretch of black earth, which was as worn and shiny as a snotty sleeve. The cokes of the ashy section had been trampled to crumbs, but bedded amongst them were flat shales, whose chalky surfaces gave this centre stretch a piebald appearance. There was no sharp division between the three sections, the ashes having been scuffed by feet at both ends.

All round the betting shop craters had been dug in the earth, and at their brims the mounds of displaced muck were patched with scraggy turf, like skins of moulting animals. The whole area was patched with scruffy grass, knotted with dead dock and sorrel, and spiked with old rose-bay spears. The skeleton of an elderberry bush had been bombarded and broken with half bricks, and all round it lay papers and cans, a saucepan, a bike frame, and a wheel-less pram.

As Billy walked up the pavement towards the betting shop he flexed his nostrils at the smell of fish and chips blowing straight down the street. He reached the waste ground and cut diagonally across it through the rough, then paused on a mound and raised his nose. He ground the two halfcrowns together in his pocket, and looked down at his black reflection in the puddle in the crater directly below him. He spat and shattered it, then took the coins out of his pocket and placed them edge to edge, rolling them into each other like two cog wheels.

'Right then, heads I take it, tails I don't.'

He pocketed one coin and tossed the other. When it fell he caught it on his right palm, slapped it into his left, and lifted the lid. The Queen.

'Shit.'

He revolved the profile slowly, getting up, upright, falling backwards, on her back, head-stand. Three quarters of a revolution.

'Right then, best o' three.'

He tossed again. Then looked between his fingers at the coin. Tails.

'One each, this is it then.'

Up it spun, ringing off the nail, a silver egg. Down. Clap. Heads.

'The bugger.'

He ran down the mound and walked across to the betting shop; a large brick shed converted from a lock-up shop. The big front window had been greened in, and on the fanlight was printed :

F. ROSE
LICENSED BETTING OFFICE.

The door was closed; a green door with a wooden knob. The knob was polished with use and the graining on the rich wood curved closely round its surface like mountain contours on a map. Billy ran his fingers round it, then stepped down and began to scuff at a ridge of grass, wedged like cartilage between two bricks on the path. The door opened and a man came out, looking back over his shoulder and shouting back inside as he swung outwards, pulling the door shut behind him and stepping down straight into Billy. He grabbed him to stop them both falling.

'Hey up young un, that's a grand place to be parked isn't it?'

He rotated Billy like a dancing partner and walked away, his shoes tapping the bricks and crunching the coke, followed by a muffled interlude as he crossed the earth to the pavement, where his footsteps, because of this interlude, seemed louder and sharper than a few seconds before, when he had walked over brick.

Billy turned the knob and opened the door. At the far end, stretching the width of the room, was a counter, mounted by a wire guard. Benches were situated round the walls and on one wall was a green felt board plastered with racing papers. Only a few strips of green showed between the pages, and from the fireplace directly opposite it looked as though felt scraps had been pinned haphazardly to the sheets. A fire was burning quietly in the grate, and over the mantelpiece, on a calendar, a jockey sat quietly on a quiet grey. In the centre of the room an old kitchen table was littered with more papers, and boxes of clean betting slips, and pencils tied to strings. A man was bending over the table writing, his pencil vertical, its string at full stretch. Another man was seated by the fire studying form, head down, elbows in his thighs, and at the board two men were pointing at the same spot on a page, murmuring and nodding together in consultation. All the men wore caps. Behind the counter a woman was pouring tea from a flask. When she lifted the cup she projected her lips towards it, and the steam made her narrow her eyes.

When Billy opened the door they all looked at him, then immediately lost interest. He took the folded slip from his pocket and smoothed it out onto the table.

'I say, mister, what price are these two?'

He showed them to the man with the tight stringed pencil, who put it down and took the slip.

'What are they?'

He began to run his forefinger swiftly down the list of runners, stopped suddenly at Crackpot, then continued slowly to the S.P. at the bottom of the race.

'Crackpot, 100–6. And Tell Him He's Dead, that's ... where is it? I've just been looking at that missen. ... Tell – Him – He's – Dead. ... 4–1, second favourite.'

He gave the slip back to Billy.

'100–6 and 4–1.'

'Have they got a chance?'

The man chuckled in his throat and shook his head.

'Nay, lad, how do I know?'

'Would you back 'em?'

The man became serious again and picked a sheet up from the table. Billy watched his face as though his calculations were being transmitted there.

'That Tell – Him – He's – Dead's got a good chance. It's top weight, but it's t'best horse in t'race. It must be, else it wouldn't be top weight would it? I don't fancy t'other though. No form. It hasn't even a jockey on it in here. It'll finish up wi' a lad on it tha can bet. No. I wouldn't bother wi' that one.'

'You don't think they'll win then?'

'How's tha got 'em, doubled?'

He lifted Billy's wrist for another look at the slip.

'They're not mine, they're our Jud's.'

'He'll be all right if they do. I can't see it missen though.' He shook his head and went back to his own selections. Billy screwed the slip up and threw it dart-style into the fire. It bounced off the crust into the hearth without catching fire. Billy went out.

The fish and chip shop was one of a parade of shops at the end of the street. It stood next to the Co-op, which curved round the corner, and bore the first number of the next road, 2 Co-operative Road. FISH F HARTLEY CHIPS. A letter tile stretching the length of the premises: a link of green letters between the shop and the upstairs flat.

F. Hartley was reading the top sheet of a pile of wrapping papers which were stacked neatly on the shelf behind the counter. Mrs Hartley was rasping flat bags off a wad and flicking her fingers inside them, opening them like carnival hats and transferring them to a baggy heap at her left side. They were both wearing white smocks, with F.H. embroidered in green on the breast pocket. There was no one else in the shop. Billy jumped up at the counter and remained hanging there by folding his arms and taking the weight on them. His toes drummed the wooden panels nearly a foot from the ground.

'A bob's worth o' chips an' a fish.'

He looked down at the upside-down page that F.H. was perusing. Still perusing it, F.H. picked it up in slow motion and placed it carefully to one side. Then he looked up at Billy's face looking over the counter close to his.

'Get down. There'll be no wood left when tha's finished banging thi feet on it.'

Billy slid down, then climbed up the queue barrier to see over the counter again.

'Serve him, Mary.'

Mary stopped opening bags and turned to the pans. She slid the lids back and shovelled a load of chips. Billy watched the scoop lifting and loading like a midget dumper. Mary reached for a fish, then paused and spoke into the mirror.

'We might as well get rid of these chips, Floyd, it's getting late now.'

Floyd didn't answer. Mary waited, watching him through the painted information, OPEN WED. DINNER, her eyes spectacled O P in the mirror.

'Can I have some scraps missus?'

Mary shovelled another dollop of chips into the bag, and topped it up, spilling them into the newspaper. Half a scoop of scraps, a tail end, and she had to use both hands to pass the big shuttlecock over the counter. Billy exchanged his half-crown, his eyes as grateful as the five thousand. A shake of salt, a shower of vinegar, and with his change in his pocket, he walked out with his portable feast.

Round the corner past the Co-op, to GEORGE BEAL FAMILY BUTCHER.

'A quarter o' beef.'

'By, them smell good.'

'Want one?'

Billy offered the packet over the counter. The Family Butcher squeezed a couple between his bloody fingers and gobbed them.

'Lovely.'

He turned to a side block, and with one stroke of the knife sliced a strip of beef clean off a joint.

'You've still got that bird then?'

He flopped the beef on to the scales and sucked his teeth while the pointer steadied. Billy felt for his money. George Beal wrapped the meat up and handed it over.

'Here, tha can have that.'

'For nowt?'

'It's only a scrap.'

'Do you want another chip?'

'No, I'll be going for my dinner in a minute.'

'Ta-ra.'

'So long.'

Billy dropped the meat into his inside pocket and walked along the shop fronts, looking into the windows: the fruiterers, apples wrapped in purple papers: the hairdressers, cardboard smilers newly permed; the HIGH CLASS GROCER at the end. He went in, ten Embassy and a box o' matches, then strolled back to school, eating his dinner.

He finished it just before he reached the gates.

Afternoon quiet. Darkening sky. Cloud skittering low in thickening hues.

The rooms along the front of the school were lighted: rooms 1 to 6, two bright blocks divided by foyer and offices. From the road, looking through the railings across the grass, silent pictures from room to room; same story, different players: the teacher at the front, the profiles of the window row. Rooms 6 and 5, teachers seated. 4, standing at the board. The Deputy's office, the Deputy at his desk. Foyer dim, deserted, like the Headmaster's room next to it. The secretary in her office, straight-backed, fingers dancing on the keys. Room 3, empty, lights left on. Room 2, Billy half-way down the row. Windows closed, top panes misting over.

The class was quiet, working; the teacher reading, looking up each time he turned a page. The atmosphere was heavy. The air stunk of sour milk and sweat. Billy eased himself down in his chair and stretched his legs under the desk. He lay his left arm along the radiator and closed his eyes.

The scuffle of a turning page. A shifting chair. A whisper. A giggle. And a cough. All isolated, exaggerated sounds.

'Casper.'

A voice from the gods.

'Casper!'

Billy sat up white-faced, staring like somebody laid too long. He stretched, fingers linked, joints going off like jumping crackers.

'Get on with your work lad.' Then back to his book.

Billy dipped his pen and leaned over his book, shading his eyes with his left hand.

Divide 42174 by 781.

Pen poised, nib pointing at the page. The ink skin in the nib-hole burst, scattered spots between the turquoise lines. Billy's eyelids began to droop. His elbow began to slide along the desk, his body after it, until the lip of the desk lid stopped his chest and made him open his eyes. He changed elbows, snuggled his shins up to the radiator and settled again, His glazed eyes fixed on the window. Clouding window. He raised his hand and drew his nib down through the cloud, scratching a course as clear as water. His hand stayed limp on the sill. The nib rusted, and the inkspots on his exercise book dried.

Jud walked slowly past the school, looking through the railings at the flickering rooms. He completed the length of the building, then turned round and came back. When he reached the main gates he turned in and walked up the drive.

Billy opened his eyes and stared at the window as though listening to it. The whole pane was obscure. He wiped a hole in the mist and peered through it. Nobody there. Just a passing car, the smudged glass blurring its outline and spangling its lamps like tears.

'Anything to report, Casper?'

Billy turned to the front.

'Never mind what's going off out there, get on with your work, lad.'

Divide 42174 by 781.

Billy looked at it, then nudged the boy beside him.

'Hey up, did tha see somebody just come up t'drive?'

He was too busy working. He shook his head. Billy prodded the boy in front.

'What?'

'Has tha seen anybody just come up t'drive?'

'I don't know, I wasn't looking.'

The boy behind. No.

Then, from the corridor side, a distant clicking, building slowly to the ringing of steel-tipped heels, making everyone look and turn in anticipation towards the sound.

Jud, looking in as he passed; out of sight, the sound dying down the corridor. The boys looked at Billy. The colour was draining from his face before their very eyes. Click Click Click Click, still audible, steady as a clock. Then stopping as suddenly; and returning. All eyes lifted to the corner by the door, watching as the sound came closer, closer, loud enough to justify an appearance many seconds before Jud's upper body actually popped into view. Looking in the length of the room. A sitting duck along the top of the cupboards. Gone.

'Wasn't that your illustrious brother, Casper?'

Billy was still staring at the corner where Jud had disappeared.

'I wouldn't have thought he was the type to pay his old school a visit.'

He started to lower his eyes to his book, then glanced up again at Billy.

'Are you all right, lad?' Pause. 'Casper. What's the matter with you? Do you feel sick?'

'No, Sir.'

'Are you sure? Do you want to go out for a drink of water or something?'

'No, Sir.'

'Open a window then, perhaps that'll make you feel better.'

'I'm all right, Sir.'

'Please yourself.'

Billy shielded his face from the rest of the class and pretended to work. Tears mingled with the sweat bobbles on the sides of his nose and sped down his cheeks. He licked them away and wiped his hand down his face.

The bell rang.

'Right, pass your books to the front. Front boy in each row bring them out.'

Billy sat back and looked round. On every desk there was an exercise book and a text-book: seventy-two books to be closed and handed in. Two seconds later they were all closed, and the relaying from the back to the front had begun. Billy's contribution was carried out in slow motion, but in spite of this, within twenty seconds of the teacher's order, all the books had been stacked into neat piles at the front of each row. They were then carried out and stacked on the teacher's desk in three piles of equal height: thirty-six exercise books in one pile, eighteen text-books in each of the other two. And the whole job completed in twenty-seven seconds.

'Right, you can go.'

Chairs were scraped back, the aisles filled up, and the class straggled out. Billy stayed put, and when the teacher made no move, he slid off his chair and fumbled about on the floor, occasionally glancing over the desk lid. The teacher closed his novel, placed it on top of the exercise books, and picked the pile up as he stood up.

'What's the matter, Casper, lost something?'

He turned away and made for the door. Billy scrambled out of his place and cut across the rows, reaching him just as he entered the corridor. He turned right. Billy's class had gone left. The last boy was twenty yards away. A few yards further on Tibbut was talking to Jud, who had his back to the notice board and one boot up against the wall. When Billy appeared Tibbut pointed to him. Jud pushed himself up and took his hands out of his pockets. Billy caught up with his teacher and tracked him closely, looking round every few steps. They turned the corner. Through the windows across the quadrangle Jud could be seen following them. While Billy was watching him, the teacher entered a classroom and closed the door. Jud turned the corner. Billy looked at him, then sprinted, dodging and banging his way the full length of the corridor, past classrooms, cloakroom, and into the toilets. He leaned back on the door. It hurried to, then slowed abruptly. He shoved it with his legs, but the air brake refused to be hurried and the door squeezed shut at its own set pace. Ear to the door, listening, eyes starting to panic. He ran straight across the toilets and out of the side door. The yard was deserted. Across the field a crow flapped sideways into the air, flapped the length of the football pitch, and landed on the crossbar. Billy flattened himself to the wall.

Inner door opening. Footsteps. Silence. Door clicking shut. Footsteps approaching. He got ready to run, then BANG, BANG, BANG, as the cubicle doors were kicked back against the walls. He ducked down and raced little-man up the side of the school under the classroom windows. 'Therefore AB must equal AC ... five fives are twenty-five, six fives are thir-ty! ... Like a wall of green glass topped with snow. The ship ...' In through the side door, pausing and peeping up and down the corridor. Empty. He walked down past the classrooms he had just passed on the outside. Mr Farthing, book before him, class intent. ... The six times table muffled through the glass. ... Mr Crossley at the board, pointing to a triangle inside a circle. ... Billy dodged into the cloakroom and ran down a corridor of coats to the far end. He listened for a minute, then unhooked a collection of raincoats, overcoats and dufflecoats, and humped them on top of each other on adjoining end pegs, forming a bulk like a tree trunk, which he disappeared into and parted slightly to spy out into the main corridor. A boy passed, picking his nose, oblivious. Billy sat on his haunches, waiting.

Waiting. No one appeared, so he emerged from his hideout, stepped down off the foot-bench and ran the few yards up to the corridor. Nobody there; just an electric buzz and an echo permeating the atmosphere. He went into the toilets next door: empty, the cubicle doors ajar at different angles. He ran across

to the outer door, and pressed a cheek to the meshed glass, trying to squint along the outside walls. His view was obstructed
by jutting brick, so he stepped back and glanced out across the
fields. The crow had flown from the crossbar. The goals ran
parallel, horizontally and vertically, to the mesh pattern in the
glass, and the posts filled the width of one mesh square exactly.

He yanked the door open and rushed out into the yard,
looking back over his shoulders at the walls. Blank. He cut
back into the wall, sneaked down to the corner and peeped
round the back of the school. Just the cycle shed, a cluster
of bins and a blunt heap of coke. He sprinted across to the
cycle shed and glanced inside. Cycles. Crept down the side and
peeped round the corner, along the back and up the far side.
Then a look across the front of the shed to his starting point,
and a wipe of his brow on his sleeve.

Somewhere in school a class was singing. They would sing
a verse then break it down : every few bars the piano would
stop, and the hoo-haa-hee of voices would tail away, dragging
the tune down with it. The same snatch would be repeated,
and repeated; until finally the whole verse would be allowed
again, the new version sounding exactly the same as the original.

Billy ran back across the asphalt and tried the boiler room
door. It opened. Hot air rushed past him out of the darkness.
The light switch was on the wall to his left. He felt sideways
for it and clicked it on. A yard inside the door the floor fell
away in a ten foot cliff. Across a chasm, at the same height as
Billy's feet, was the top of the boiler. A good long-jumper could
have run from the cycle shed, straight in, and jumped on top of
it. From the boiler, pipes bent up the walls and disappeared
through the ceiling like branches of the beanstalk. The whitewashed walls were grey with dust, and a thickness of dust lay
like fur around the shoulder of the bulb, which was suspended
on a long flex from the ceiling.

Billy stepped to the cliff edge, turned around and descended
the iron ladder. The edges of the rungs were rusty. The centres
were hollowed and silver with wear.

In the well bottom, the boiler occupied most of the floor
space. Billy flicked his fingers at the insulating coat surround-

ing it, tigging it as though expecting it to be red hot. It was warm, a pleasant heat, like a hot water bottle wrapped in a towel. He walked down one side. At the back, between the boiler and the wall, was a yard gap, spanned in the centre by a thick pipe at ground level. He skiddled back up the side of the boiler, back up the ladder, and shut himself in. Clicked the light off, then stood still, waiting for the black shapes to come out and establish themselves in the darkness. Then back down the ladder to the space behind the boiler, where he sat down and rested his head against the pipe; as snug as a bug, as warm as toast, as safe as houses; enclosed on two sides, with the darkness before him and the thick pipe behind. He began to nod.

When he woke up the light was on, and somebody was moving about close by. He sat still, staring down at his pumps which were sticking out in the shadow of the boiler. Holding his breath he flexed his knees and withdrew them, replacing them close to his buttocks. Then, pushing himself up on his finger tips, he transferred his weight forward from his heels to his toes, and rocked over to a cat-landing on all fours. A pause for listening, then he peeped round the corner of the boiler. The caretaker was feeling into a jacket hanging on a nail in the wall. He found a twenty cigarette packet, shook it, and turned away. As he ascended the ladder the studs in his boots made music on the metal. He clicked the light off and swung the door to. The band of sky in the doorway narrowed rapidly, and on the walls, darkness slid across the panels of light like a curtain.

Billy stood up and stretched. He padded up the ladder, felt for the door sneck and pulled. Stuck. Pulled and rattled. Locked.

'Bloody hell.'

He dabbed for the lock, grabbed it, felt it with his finger tips, and smiled. Yale.

The wind had dropped. It was starting to rain. Big spots dotted the asphalt like pennies from heaven. On top of the cycle shed a black cat froze in mid-stride and stared down at him. When he shut the door the noise and movement sent it silently down the grain of the tin and out of sight down the back of the shed.

It was quiet without the wind. No birds sang, and the singing had stopped in school. There was no sound from the school. Billy stood back in the doorway listening, and watching the back corner of the shed. Nothing happened. So he ran across and had a look. The cat had gone. On the roof of the shed the raindrops were quickening like a heartbeat. The sound developed into a solo, and water began to trickle down the tin, bringing up the rust, copper and orange. Billy turned round and sprinted. Round the corner of the building, straight in through the toilets and into the corridor. Empty. The first classroom he looked into was empty. The second was occupied. He stared in until he attracted everyone's attention, and the teacher came rushing to the door.

'What's the matter, Casper? What are you looking at?'

'What time is it, Sir?'

'Time! Never mind the time lad! What do you want?'

He stepped down the corridor. Billy stepped back.

'Is this 3B, Sir?'

'No it isn't 3B, why?'

'I thought it wa'. I've got a message for 'em.'

'Well get to the office then.'

'Why, are they in there, Sir?'

'No, to find out where they are, you fool! Ask the secretary to look at the timetable.'

'Yes, Sir. I forgot.'

'You will forget, lad, if you come disturbing me again like that.'

He banged the door and frowned his way across to his desk. He was still frowning when he resumed the lesson, two vertical frowns between his eyes. Billy walked slowly by and looked into the next room. A class was working. He dodged back out of sight and stood between the two rooms with his back to the radiator, glancing continually right and left, up and down the corridor.

The bell rang, and before the ringing had stopped doors opened and boys came out into the corridor. For the first few seconds there were wide spaces between them, but these spaces diminished rapidly as the rooms emptied and whole classes

merged, shouting and jostling, and pursuing their various destinations. Billy shouted and jostled with them. 'Seen 4c? Hey up!
Seen our class?' Jumping up to see over heads; failing, and
mounting boys' backs to gain a momentary vantage point. They
tried to wrestle and thump him off, but he was too quick, and
he jumped down and dodged away while they were still bent
forward.

He found them and rushed amongst them, smiling and rubbing
shoulders. 'Where's tha been, Casper?' Billy just smiled and
mingled, and moved alongside Tibbut.

'Seen our Jud?'

'Hey up, where's tha been? They've been looking all over for
thee.'

'Who has?'

'Gryce pudding and everybody.'

'What for? I haven't done owt.'

'Youth Employment. Tha should have gone for thi interview
last lesson.'

'Seen our Jud?'

'I saw him earlier on, why?'

'Did he say owt?'

'Just asked where tha wa' that's all. What did tha run away
for when tha saw him?'

'Seen him since?'

'What's up, is he after thi for summat?'

When they reached their classroom Gryce was standing at
the door. When he saw Billy he batted him twice about the ears,
forehand left ear, backhand right.

'And where do you think you've been, lad?'

Billy muffed his ears with his hands.

'Nowhere, Sir,' shouting like someone deaf.

'Nowhere! Don't talk ridiculous lad! Who are you, the invisible man?'

Billy backed into the empty room as Gryce came for him
again.

'I felt sick, Sir. I went to the toilet.'

'And where were you, down it? I sent prefects to the toilets
they said you weren't there.'

'I went outside then, Sir. For a breath o' fresh air.'

'I'll give you fresh air.'

Billy manoeuvred a horseshoe course, to stay within striking distance of the door.

'I've just come back in, Sir.'

'And what about your interview? I've had the whole school out looking for you.'

'I'm just goin', Sir.'

'Well get off then! And God help anyone who employs you.'

Billy set off, then stopped in mid-stride and half turned.

'Where to Sir?'

'The medical room! If you'd stay awake in assembly you'd know where to!'

He lunged across and made another swipe. But Billy had gone, and he overbalanced and staggered, like a tennis player failing to make a forehand return. The audience, observing through the doorway and the corridor windows, turned away and stared into space, not daring to meet each other's eyes. Gryce parted them like a curtain and strode away up the corridor, massaging his shoulder. He stopped massaging to cuff a small boy on the back of the head and shove him to one side.

'Get over, lad! Don't you know to keep to the right hand side yet?'

There were four chairs outside the medical room. A woman and a boy occupied the two nearest the door. Billy sat down, leaving an empty chair between them. The boy leaned forward and nodded at him across the front of the woman. The woman glanced round, then turned back to the boy.

'And don't be sat there like a dummy when you get in there.'

The boy blushed and looked across at Billy again. Billy sat staring straight ahead, top teeth working across his bottom lip, squeezing it white.

'Tell him that you're after a good job, an office job, summat like that.'

'Who's after an office job?'

'Well what are you after then? A job on t'bins?'

'I wish you'd shut up.'

'An' straighten your tie.'

The boy held the knot and pulled the back tag. The knot slid up and covered the top button of his clean white shirt. 'I wish you'd stop nagging.'

'Somebody's to nag.'

The door opened. The woman stood up and practised a smile down at herself. A boy emerged, followed by a woman smiling back into the room. The women smiled at each other. Their boys grinned. They crossed. The door closed, and the interviewed couple walked away, close in conversation. They stepped in accord, but the clip of high-heels predominated, and their echo preceded them down the corridor. Billy watched them go, then propped his face in his hands and stared down between his legs.

The floor was covered with red and green vinyl tiles set in a check pattern. Their surfaces were mottled white, seeking a marble effect. On some tiles the mottling was severe, on others a mere fleck, and where a series of heavily mottled tiles had been laid together, the white dominated the basic colours as though something had been spilt there.

Billy placed his feet parallel over two edges of the red tile directly between his legs. They just failed to span the tile's length. He eased his heels back to the corner, increasing the space at his toes. Then he eased them forward, decreasing the toe space, but introducing a growing space at his heels. He wriggled his toes, trying to stretch his feet, his pumps rippling like caterpillars. But the space remained constant, so he lifted his feet and perched them out of sight on the stretcher under the chair.

The white markings of the red tile, and the markings of the adjoining green ones never matched up; they all missed slightly, like a fault in a stratum of rock. The only strokes that did cross the dividing lines were skid marks made by rubber-soled shoes. These skid marks scarred all the tiles, and ranged from blunt scuffs to long sabres. They all pointed lengthways down the corridor, but were so different in form that they were never quite parallel to each other, or to the lanes formed by the edges of the tiles.

Billy sat back and lifted his head. On the opposite wall, directly across from the Medical Room door, was a fire alarm. Underneath it, in red capitals, were the instructions, IN CASE OF FIRE BREAK GLASS. The case of the alarm was red painted metal. The glass was round, like a big watch face. Billy sat and stared at it. A woman laughed close by. He turned instinctively towards the sound, then stood up and walked across to the alarm. Behind the glass, almost touching it, was a knob. Billy ran a finger round the rim, gathering dust under the nail. He breathed on the glass, drew a Union Jack in the vapour, then rubbed it up with his cuff. The glass shone. He tinked it with his nails, tapped it with a knuckle, then rapped it with his knuckles. The noise made him step back and glance up and down the corridor. All quiet. Nobody there. Then the door opened. Billy swung round. Boy. Woman. Man at desk behind, between them. 'Good afternoon.' Left masking the alarm, looking across, in at the bald crust of a man writing. He looked up, out at Billy.

'Are you next?'

Billy looked in, not moving.

'Well come in, lad, if you're coming, I haven't got all day.'

Billy walked in, closed the door and crossed the room.

'Sit down, Walker.'

'I'm not Walker.'

'Well who are you then? According to my list it should be Gerald Walker next.'

He checked his name list.

'Oliver, Stenton, then Walker.'

'I'm Casper.'

'Casper. O yes. I should have seen you earlier, shouldn't I?' He flicked through the record cards. 'Casper.... Casper.... here we are,' placed it on top, then replaced the stack on the blotting square.

'Mmm.'

While he studied Billy's card, Billy studied his scalp. The crown was clean and pink. Hair, cut short and neat, grew round the back and sides, and a few greased strands had been carefully combed across the front to disguise the baldness. But they failed, like a trap covered with inadequate foliage.

'Now then, Casper, what kind of job had you in mind?'

He shunted the record cards to one side, and replaced them with a blank form, lined and sectioned for the relevant information. CASPER, WILLIAM, in red on the top line. He copied age, address and other details from the record card, then changed pens and looked up.

'Well?'

'I don't know, I haven't thought about it right.'

'Well you should be thinking about it. You want to start off on the right foot, don't you?'

'I suppose so.'

'You haven't looked round for anything yet then?'

'No, not yet.'

'Well what would you like to do? What are you good at?'

He consulted Billy's record card again.

'Offices held.... Aptitudes and Abilities ... right then ... would you like to work in an office? Or would you prefer manual work?'

'What's that, manual work?'

'It means working with your hands, for example, building, farming, engineering. Jobs like that, as opposed to pen pushing jobs.'

'I'd be all right working in an office, wouldn't I? I've a job to read and write.'

The Employment Officer printed MANUAL on the form, then raised his pen hand as though he was going to print it again on the top of his head. He scratched it instead, and the nails left white scratches on the skin. He smoothed his fingers carefully across the plot of hair, then looked up. Billy was staring straight past him out of the window.

'Have you thought about entering a trade as an apprentice? You know, as an electrician, or a bricklayer or something like that. Of course the money isn't too good while you're serving your apprenticeship. You may find that lads of your own age who take dead end jobs will be earning far more than you; but in those jobs there's no satisfaction or security, and if you do stick it out you'll find it well worth your while. And whatever happens, at least you'll always have a trade at your finger tips won't you? ...

'Well, what do you think about it? And as you've already said you feel better working with your hands, perhaps this would be your best bet. Of course this would mean attending Technical College and studying for various examinations, but nowadays most employers encourage their lads to take advantage of these facilities, and allow them time off to attend, usually one day a week. On the other hand, if your firm wouldn't allow you time off in the day, and you were still keen to study, then you'd have to attend classes in your own time. Some lads do it. Some do it for years, two and three nights a week from leaving school, right up to their middle twenties, when some of them take their Higher National, and even degrees.

'But you've got to if you want to get on in life. And they'll all tell you that it's worth it in the end.... Had you considered continuing your education in any form after leaving? ... I say, are you listening, lad?'

'Yes.'

'You don't look as though you are to me. I haven't got all day you know, I've other lads to see before four o'clock.'

He looked down at Billy's form again.

'Now then, where were we? O, yes. Well if nothing I've mentioned already appeals to you, and if you can stand a hard day's graft, and you don't mind getting dirty, then there are good opportunities in mining ...'

'I'm not goin' down t'pit.'

'Conditions have improved tremendously ...'

'I wouldn't be seen dead down t'pit.'

'Well what do you want to do then? There doesn't seem to be a job in England to suit you.'

He scrutinized Billy's record card again as though there might be a hint of one there.

'What about hobbies? What hobbies have you got? Do you like gardening, or constructing Meccano sets, or anything like that?'

Billy shook his head slowly.

'Don't you have any hobbies at all?'

Billy looked at him for a moment, then stood up quickly.

'Can I go now?'

'What's the matter with you, lad? Sit down, I haven't finished yet.'

Billy remained standing. The Youth Employment Officer began to fill in the blanks on the form, quickly and noisily.

'Well I've interviewed some lads in my time, but I've never met one like you. Half the time you're like a cat on hot bricks, the other half you're not even listening.'

He turned the form face down on the blotter and ran the sides of his fist along it, continuing the stroke off the blotter and pinching a blue leaflet off a wad at the front of the desk.

'Here, take this home and read it. It gives you all the relevant information concerned with school leaving and starting work. Things like sickness benefits, National Insurance, etcetera. At the back,' he turned it over and pointed at it, 'there's a detachable form. When you want your cards, fill it in and send it in to the office. The address is given at the top. Have you got that?'

Billy stared at the leaflet and nodded.

'Well take it then.... And if you do have trouble getting fixed up, don't forget, come in and see me. All right?'

The pamphlet was entitled LEAVING SCHOOL. The text on the cover page was built around a sketch which showed a man in square glasses shaking hands across a desk with a strapping youth in blazer and flannels. Their mouths were all teeth. Through the window behind the man was a tree, and a flying V bird.

'Right, Casper, that's all. Tell the next boy to come in.'

When he got out he started to run. He ran straight out of school and all the way home.

The shed door was open. The hawk was gone. The hasp was still locked to the door jamb, but the four screws which had secured it to the door hung useless in the metal plate. On the door the plate had left a pale impression like a turned stone in a field, and where the screws had been prised from their sockets, the wood was splintered and bruised. Billy rushed into the shed, rushed out again, and rushed round the back up onto the fence.

'Kes! Kes!'

He jumped down and ran up the path, barged into the kitchen door, and bounced back when it wouldn't open.

'Jud!'

He felt under the step for the key, fumbled it into the lock, and rushed in.

The curtains were still closed in the living-room. Light filtered through the kitchen, through the doorway, and across the lino like a third-hand strip of carpet. He ran across the living-room and opened the door into the hall. It was lighter there, the top panel of the front door was frosted glass. He fell forward on to the bottom steps and shouted up the stairs.

'Jud! Jud!'

The echo was snubbed as he scrambled on all fours up the stairs. The back bedroom door was open. It was quiet and dark inside. Billy stepped into the room, holding on to the door-jamb with one hand.

'Jud.'

He switched the light on. The bed was exactly as it had been left that morning; the pillows were buckled, the blankets rutted, and the thrown back sheet pointed at him like a thrust out tongue. He skiddled back down the stairs, back through the living-room into the kitchen; and paused a moment on the trestle to scan across the fields and the sky.

The sky had hardened into one charcoal shell. Beyond the nearest field all distance was lost, and in the failing light no birds were visible. No birds called, and the only sound was the hum of the rain.

Billy ran into the garage, fetched the lure from his bag, and began to unwind it and swing it as he hurried down the garden and climbed over the fence.

'Kes! Kes! Come on then Kes!'

He patrolled the field, calling continuously, working the lure and changing hands until he could work it no longer, and he had to let it drop out of sight in the grass. He stood looking round for a few seconds, then started to run, the lure bouncing behind him as he wound it in. He vaulted back into the garden, and ran up the side of the house to the front gate. A woman was approaching up the far pavement. Every time she walked behind a parked car, her head looked as though it was travelling along a conveyer belt. There was no one else in sight. Billy ran across the road and surprised her by bobbing out in front of a car.

'Oo! You dozy young devil. You scared me to death.'

'Have you seen our Jud anywhere down there?'

He nodded away down the avenue.

'Your Jud? No, I haven't seen him, why?'

She watched Billy run away up the pavement, then took her hand away from her heart and walked after him, head bowed against the rain.

'Ee, what a family that is.'

The bookmaker's wife was just locking up when Billy reached the edge of the waste ground.

'Hey! Mrs Rose!'

She glanced round, then turned the key and opened her handbag.

'Have you seen our Jud?'

She squeezed the clasps, CLICK, and started down the path, Billy following.

'I can see you haven't, else you wouldn't be in one piece now.'

'You've seen him then?'

'Seen him? He nearly ripped t'place apart that's all.'

'Have you seen him since?'

'Called me all t'names under t'sun. Called me a welcher, and said I was trying to rob his eyes out. Then he threatened Tommy Leach wi' violence when he tried to put a word in. We had a right pantomime. I'd to send for Eric Clough and Eric Street in t'end to prove that you never placed that bet.'

'Has he been back?'

'They both won you know. Crackpot got a hundred to eight. Tell Him He's Dead got fours. He'd have had over a tenner to draw.'

'Do you know where he is now?'

'Why didn't you put it on?'

'How do I know? I didn't know they were goin' to win did I?'

He started to cry. Mrs Rose shook her head.

'You won't half cop it, lad, when he gets hold of you.'

They had reached the Co-op at the end of the street. Billy stopped and Mrs Rose walked away from him. He turned and ran back the way they had come, back past the betting shop. Back across the estate, down the avenue into the cul-de-sac, and through the snicket into the fields.

A few yards along the path, and the houses had faded from dull red to dark shapes in the dusk. Only the silhouette of their roofs showed clearly against the sky. Billy pulled the lure from his inside pocket, and searched in his other pockets for his handkerchief. He found it, and flapped it open, then he tied it to the lure and began to swing it as he continued slowly along the path.

'Kes! Kes! Come on then Kes!'

He looked upwards all the time, meandering off the path into the grass, back on to the path, through puddles and sludge; wiping the sludge away as he meandered back into the grass.

'Come on Kes! Come on then!'

At first the handkerchief twirled and dipped behind the lure as crisp as a kite-tailing, but the rain and the wet grass quickly transformed it into a sodden grey rag flapping in the gloom.

Round and round, so fast that the cord sang; slower, to rest and change hands. Then shortening the cord and whirring it so that the cord and the lure and the rag fused like a Catherine wheel, and unwound as a rocket as he released it, and it shot up into the sky, slowed, spent itself, and fell back to the ground. He ran to retrieve it, and immediately swung it back into action.

'Kes! Kes! Kes!'

His call was pitching up to a scream. He was panting and sobbing, but each time he shortened his grip on the cord to increase the momentum of the lure, he held his breath. He held it each time the lure travelled up; and there was silence until it fell back unattended, and he ran forward to pick it up, crying.

At the end of the field a stile spanned the gap in the hedgerow. The two posts were cold and slimy to the touch. Billy climbed the two steps, then, holding on to the posts, climbed up on to the cross-piece, and slowly, very carefully, with the outsides of his feet pressed against the verticals, he straightened up, balancing like the top man of a pyramid of tumblers. Taller than the hedgerow, he stared round. On both sides and before him, fences and hedges were black borders for grey blankets. He stared hard into the distance to where the woods should be, then turned round, and the rotation of his trunk almost fetched him off backwards. He grabbed a post, steadied himself, then slowly began to swing the lure.

In the dusk, feet braced, above the fields, he swung the lure, calling, calling, calling. Sometimes the lure smacked the hedge, momentarily destroying his balance and the rhythm of his swing. But with a flex of the knees and a sway of the hips, he adjusted his stance and brought the lure back into play. Sometimes the handkerchief dragged across the hawthorn spikes, ripping it a little each time, until finally it ripped away from the lure and lay spiked on the hedge top. Billy left it, a dark shape on the hedge; a shade of the hedge, like the lure passing over the hedge, and emerging a mere silhouette in the gloom.

Billy let the lure fall in front of him, and stepped down after it; swinging it up again and continuing along the path towards the woods. The face of the woods began to come up out of the gloom, a black band stretching right and left, and filling more of the sky as he walked towards it. The lure, when swung vertically to its limit, surmounted the raggy silhouette of the trees, and for a second imposed itself against the greyer sky, before diving, and bumping the ground and being pulled up on a flatter trajectory. But as Billy neared the trees, he reached a point where no matter how steeply he swung it, the lure failed to clear the tree tops and stayed ineffective against a total background.

He started to run. He reached the stile leading into the woods and ran over it, dragging the lure behind him. It caught on the cross-bar and jerked him to a halt. He tugged it, wound the cord round his hand and rushed forward. The cord broke, releasing him staggering forward off balance; regaining balance, and shaking the loose cord away from his hand as he left the path and cut into the undergrowth.

'Kes! Kes! Kes! Kes!'

It was immediately darker, and he had to move with his arms forward to protect his face from the branches of the saplings. Above the saplings were the dark bunches of the hawthorns, and high above these the branches of the tallest trees formed lattice work against the sky.

He blundered on, shouting into the darkness, stumbling and falling on all fours, resting a moment with head down like a tired animal, then scrambling up and on again. He came out of the undergrowth into the heart of the wood, where there was more space between the trees, and each space was as damp and dark as a cellar. The leaf mould gave beneath his tread, and where the leaves had been gathered in hollows and at the bottom of slopes by the Autumn winds, his feet disappeared completely; sinking, high stepping, slow motion skating when his legs got tired, and stopping when the drifts reached up to his knees. When he stopped he called, and waited, but the only sounds were the echo of his voice and the rain.

The rain, millions of drops per second, some falling between the branches, some hitting the branches, where they fused and gathered underneath as heavier drops, until their weight parted them from the branches – splash – into the rotting mould. To be replaced by identical pendant drops. All over the woods, from millions of branches, millions of drops per second, pat pat pat against the background hiss of the rain falling straight through.

'Kes! Kes! Kes!'

The one syllable of the call was echoed in the pat of the drops: a whisper all through the woods as Billy progressed. Dying under each fresh call, but picking it up immediately, more subtle, more insistent than the call itself. He brushed against an oak sapling, still thick with dead leaves. They rattled like snakes, making him veer away, anywhere, running, calling, tripping and falling over stumps and branches clogged down under matted grass. He hit the path again, crossed into the other side of the wood and back-tracked, coming out at the stile where he had first entered. It was dark across the fields. In the distance the sky had an orange tint as though the estate was on fire. Billy cut back into the trees, straight into a bramble patch. He ran on, his initial impetus carrying him the first few yards, before the tentacles started to bind on his jeans, dragging at the material and cutting through his socks at the ankles. Slower and slower, until he was sprinting dead slow as though in a nightmare. Sprinting on the spot, then stopping and stamping his way out.

He covered ground he had already covered. He crossed ridings to cover new ground, then recrossed them to cover the old ground again all without plan, because it was too dark to take bearings from the trees or any other form of marker.

Until finally the trees thinned, and through them he could see the lights of the Monastery Farm. He made towards them, coming out of the trees at the hedge which skirted the cart track separating the woods from the farm. In the house the kitchen curtains were open and the light shone out on to the lawn and the stumpy apple trees dotted about it. To the right of the house the stables and other outhouses could be picked out by the lights from the yard behind them, and just apart from these buildings, in the dark, was the vague hulk of the barn. To the left of the house was an open space where the monastery wall had stood. The site was clear now, except for a few slabs of tumbled masonry which could be made out as dark shapes amongst the grass. Billy stared over the hedge across at the farm for a long time. Then he started to shiver and turned away, and slowly made his way back through the woods.

Something rustled and ran before him, disturbing a bird into flight through the branches.

'Kes!'

He found the path and followed it back to the stile. As he climbed over, his legs touched the broken lure line. He unwound it from the cross-bar, rewound it round the lure, then jumped down and started to run back across the fields towards the estate.

The houses came up as a link of black cut-outs against an orange background. Lighted windows made a sequence of coloured squares along the bottom of the shapes, but this sequence was broken by the sudden illumination of a bedroom window, off-set from the lighted window below it.

Billy reached the houses and ran up the snicket into the cul-de-sac; into the orange light, which stood in fuzzy haloes round the heads of the three lamps grouped there, and round the heads of the lamps alternatively spaced up both sides of the avenue.

Their living-room light was on. Billy ran down the path, round to the kitchen door and pressed the handle, paused, then allowed it to spring back as he turned away from the door and tried to see through the darkness down to the shed. Slowly he walked towards it, slower and slower, almost stopping, then sprinting the last ten yards. The door was still open. The shed was still empty.

When Billy burst through from the kitchen his mother and Jud were half standing at the table, startled up by the clatter which had preceded his appearance. When they saw who it was they both sat down again.

'Where is it? What's tha done wi' it?'

Jud glanced up at him, then back to the comic which was propped up against the sugar basin. His mother shook her head.

'An' where you been in this lot? Just look at you, you're sodden.'

It was warm in the room. The fire was high in the grate, the radio was playing, and the tea was on the table.

'Go an' get them wet things off, then come an' get some tea.'

She opened a magazine and folded it inside out along the spine.

'An' shut that door, Billy, there's a terrible draught behind you.'

Billy stood still, still breathing heavily, looking at Jud all the time.

'I said where is it?'

Jud took no notice of him. Directly before him, equidistant between the edge of the cloth and the comic was a pot of tea. At the side of the pot stood a cylinder of biscuits, taller and thinner than the pot. Wisps of steam rose from the tea, and every few seconds Jud's exhalations blew the wisps over the slope of the comic. The whole effect was reminiscent of a model for a new industrial plant.

Jud continued to read, automatically taking biscuits from the packet and dipping them into the tea, then popping the whole darkened circles into his mouth just before they had time to disintegrate. He scoffed four biscuits in this way, and with the fifth immersed looked up at Billy, who was still watching him.

'What thar staring at?'

His shout made Mrs Casper jump. He withdrew his biscuit hurriedly. Too late, it disintegrated under his pull back into the tea, leaving a damp segment between his finger and thumb.

'Nar look what tha's made me do!'

Billy rushed to the table. His mother jumped up and swiped at him with the magazine.

'What's goin' off? What's all this bloody shouting about?'

Billy dodged the magazine easily, simultaneously answering his mother and pointing at Jud.

'Ask him, he knows what it's about!'

Jud stood up and thumped at Billy across the table.

'Yes lad, an' tha'd have known if I'd have got hold of thi earlier.'

'Known what? What you both talking about?'

She sat down, her nylon smock swishing as she crossed her legs.

'Sit down, Billy. An' get them wet things off before you catch your death.'

Billy started to cry, big sobs that took his breath.

'Now then what's a matter wi' you?'

He couldn't answer. He just pointed at Jud, who looked away, then sat and lowered his head to his comic.

'What you done to him now, Jud?'

Jud backhanded the comic straight off the table and shot up, making his mother sit up straight in her chair, and Billy stop sobbing for a moment. The exposed sugar basin stood directly beneath the light bulb. Stuck to its walls was a crust of dried sugar, dull in comparison to the sparkling white sugar in the bottom of the bowl.

'It's his fault! If he'd have put that bet on like he wa' told there'd have been none o' this!'

'An' didn't he? Well I told him before I went to work this morning.'

'Did he bloody hell.'

'I told you not to forget, Billy.'

'He didn't forget, he kept t'money.'

'An' what happened, did they win?'

'Win! I'd have had a tenner to draw if he'd kept his thieving hands to his sen!'

'A tenner! Oo, Billy, you've done it once too often this time.'

From their own sides of the table they looked across at Billy.

'Hundred to eight and four to one they came in. I knew it an' all! Tell-Him-He's-Dead was a cert, and I've been following that Crackpot all season. It wa' forced to win sometime. They were just waiting for a price that's all.'

He walked away from the table as though his loss was too great to bear standing still.

'Ten quid. I could have had a week off work wi' that.'

He picked the poker up and smashed it down on to the fire, flushing a shower of sparks up the chimney back.

'I'd have bloody killed him if I'd have got hold of him this afternoon.'

'Well, what's he crying about then?'

'Because he's killed my hawk instead, that's why!'

Jud continued to broddle in the fire.

'You haven't have you, Jud?'

'He has! I know he has! Just because he couldn't catch me!'

'Have you, Jud?'

He swung round, holding the poker like the *Daily Express* knight.

'All right then! So I've killed it! What you goin' to do about it?'

Billy rushed round the table to his mother and tried to bury his face in her. She held him off, embarrassed.

'Gi'o'er then, Billy, don't be so daft.'

'It wa' its own stupid fault! I wa' only goin' to let it go, but it wouldn't get out o' t'hut. An' every time I tried to shift it, it kept lashing out at my hands wi' its claws. Look at 'em, they're scratched to ribbons!'

He held them out for inspection. Billy ran at him, aiming

straight between them. Jud raised the poker, then pushed him away with his other hand.

'You bastard! You big rotten bastard!'

'Don't call me a bastard, else tha'll be t'next to get it.'

'You bastard! You fuckin' bastard!'

Billy stood his ground, then turned at the cuff from his mother.

'Shut up, Billy! I'm not havin' that kind o' language in here!'

'Well do summat then! Do summat to him!'

She just stood there, looking over him at Jud.

'Where is it, Jud? What you done wi' it?'

He turned away to the fireplace and replaced the poker flat in the hearth.

'It's in t'bin.'

Billy broke from between them, out through the kitchen to the dustbin at the side of the garage. He yanked the lid off and peered down. It was black inside so he reached down, fingers feeling lightly amongst the rubbish. Then he stopped feeling, and straightened up quickly, holding the hawk in his hand.

He carried it into the kitchen and stood with his back to the living-room door to inspect it. Brown eyes open. Glass eyes. Curved beak ajar, tongue just visible in the slit. Head lolling downwards, swinging whichever way he turned it to brush away the dust and ashes from the feathers. Blowing the feathers clean, raising them with his breath, then smoothing them gently into place with his fingers.

He opened one wing like a fan, and on the underside of it, slowly drew a finger down the primaries, down to the body, as though the wing was a feathered instrument, its note too soft for human hearing. He refolded the wing carefully across its back, then carried it through to the living-room.

Jud was standing with his back to the fire. His mother was standing at the table, pouring tea. The comic was still on the floor.

'Look what he's done, mam! Look at it!'

He held the hawk out to her across the table, yellow legs upwards, jesses dangling, its claws hooks in the air.

'I know, it's a shame, love; but I don't want it.'

She sat down, bringing her face on a level with the hawk.

'Look at it, though! Look what he's done!'

She looked at it, curling her top lip, then turned to Jud.

'It wa' a rotten trick, Jud.'

'It wa' a rotten trick what he did, wasn't it?'

'I know, but you know how much he thought about that bird.'

'He didn't think half as much about it as I did about that ten quid.'

'He thought world on it though. Take it away from t'table then, Billy.'

'It wasn't worth ten quid was it?'

'I know, but it wa' a rotten trick all t'same. Take it away from my face then, Billy, I've seen it.'

Billy tried to get close to her with the bird, but she wouldn't let him.

'It's not fair on him, mam! It's not fair.'

'I know it's not, but it's done now so there's nowt we can do about it is there?'

'What about him though? What you goin' to do to him? I want you to do summat to him.'

'What can I do?'

'Hit him! Gi' him a good hiding! Gi' him some fist!'

Jud snorted and turned round to look at himself in the mirror above the mantelpiece.

'I'd like to see her.'

'Talk sense, Billy, how can I hit him?'

'You never do owt to him! He gets away wi' everything!'

'O! Shut up now then! You've cried long enough about it.'

'You're not bothered about owt you.'

'Course I'm bothered. But it's only a bird. You can get another can't you?'

She looked down at her magazine and raised her cup. Billy clenched his free hand and swung at it, fisting it clean off its handle across the room, shooting out a tongue of tea. Jud, watching the scene through the mirror, was too slow to interpret the reverse order of events, and before he had time to turn or step aside both cup and tea hit him smack between the shoulder blades. Mrs Casper was left looking at the lug crooked on her finger. Billy followed the tea and the cup on to Jud's back, grasping him round the neck with both arms. Jud swung him round like a maypole hanger. Mrs Casper jumped up and tried to drag him off. He kicked out at her like a hare, and she doubled up back into the table holding her breasts. The pot wobbled. The packet of biscuits and the milk bottle fell over. The bottle rolled off the table and smashed. The biscuits were stopped by the swamp of milk on the cloth.

Billy was screaming and crying into Jud's ears. Jud was trying to reach over and grasp him by the hair, but every time his hand came back Billy swayed backwards or sideways out of its reach. Then, with a quick duck Jud flicked him over his head. Billy kept hold until the impetus of his somersaulting body made him let go, and he swung over to land knees and chest against the back of the settee, knocking it over, making the front castors squeal and spin, and revealing the pouched hessian bottom. They both went for him. Billy stood up, and, holding the hawk by the feet, swung it at them. Its wings opened, and the open eyes and the rush of feathers before their faces halted them long enough for Billy to hurdle the upturned settee and dart out between them, banging both doors behind him.

As he ran up the path to the front gate, neighbours clustered at half open doors, and at their own front gates to watch him. He jumped up on the the wall, down to the pavement and bent down at the gutter, feeling in the running water for a stone or a pebble.

'Billy! Billy, come back here!'

He turned at the voice. His mother was run-walking up the path, glancing around at all the neighbours as she came. She reached the gate, but before she had time to open it, Billy was away, up the avenue. She stood gripping the pointed verticals, watching him into the distance.

'Billy! Come back here, you young bugger!'

'You'll not catch me! You'll never catch me.'

He had been out of sight a long time before she went in. And even though it was still raining, not until she had closed the door behind her did anyone make a move to return to their own homes, or close their own doors.

Billy looked over his shoulder, then gradually eased down to a walk, as though he had just completed a long distance race. He was panting hard, but he didn't stop to rest, but continued to walk slowly down the middle of the road. There was little traffic about, and when a car did come, he just stepped aside momentarily to let it pass. He raised his right arm to wipe his face on the sleeve, and the hawk was there before his eyes, still clenched in his hand. He moved to the kerb and stopped under a lamp. When he changed hands, the palm of his right hand was hot and sweaty, and the breast feathers of the hawk were damp and matted. He stroked them back into place, stroked its back and wings, then opened his jacket and carefully placed it in the big inside pocket. There was no bulge when the jacket hung down again. He wiped his hands on his jeans and started to walk again; reached the end of the road, and without looking up, turned right into the next road, and continued head down, down its centre.

On both sides of this road, and the next, and along all the Roads, Streets, Avenues, Lanes and Crescents of the estate, the houses were of the same design : semi-detached, one block, four front windows to a block, and a central chimney stack. This pattern was occasionally broken by groups of pensioners' bungalows, tucked into Closes, but built of the same red brick as all the other dwellings.

At the front of each house was a square of garden, separated from its neighbour by a wire mesh fence, strung between concrete posts. Most of the gardens were uncultivated squares of stamped soil, or overgrown with old vegetation, and many of the fences had been climbed over and burrowed under to such an extent that they had assumed the proportions of saloon doors. Some of the fences had been completely destroyed, leaving only the four concrete posts as useless dividers.

Dividing the gardens from the pavement was a wall three feet high, built of the same brick as the houses. The top course of bricks had been laid edgeways to form a strong neat finish, but on many of the walls odd bricks had been prised out, leaving a gap like an extracted tooth. One missing brick quickly encouraged another, leading up to a whole series of removals, and at a few houses V-shaped sections had been torn away, and the gaps utilized as unofficial paths. These paths all followed a similar pattern, cutting diagonally across the gardens, to converge with the concrete paths at the house corner. The misplaced bricks lay in tumbled heaps in the shadow of the wall bottoms.

A few of the front walls were protected by a cushion of privet, and the wire divisions fortified by hedges. Between the hedges there was always a little lawn, often fashioned into a complicated design: the corners snipped off, or a triangular, circular, or star-shaped bed cut out of the centre, and in one case two corners had been cut off, and a diagonal strip led across the centre to the other two. Then there was crazy paving, and stone bird baths with stone birds drinking at their rims. There was painted trellis work, and sets of pots made from drainage pipes. There were gnomes and storks and spotted toadstools, all illuminated in unnatural shades, and casting cross-shadows from the street lamps and the squares of lighted windows. These gardens had gates, many did not, and of the ones that did, some were minus one or more of their composite palings.

Garages were common, and occasionally the corresponding cars were parked at the kerb edges. Between the kerb and the pavement a strip of soil had been laid, and at regular intervals up all the thoroughfares, black iron discs, stuck into the soil, stated, in raised capitals: SEEDED VERGES PLEASE KEEP OFF. Some of the cars were parked with their near side wheels on the verges. Some of the discs had been flattened flush to the soil like gravestones, and everywhere the soil was rutted and shiny with wear. Stuck to it were paper and cigarette packets, half bricks and dog shit, and planted in it, at fifty yard intervals, were saplings surrounded by guards of spiked railings. Few of these trees had been allowed to grow taller than the railings, and most of them were just centre spikes inside the guards. The cylinders of close fitting spikes had however been utilized as waste paper baskets, and bottles and old toys, boxes and bicycle parts had been tossed over their points to rest in tangled shadows round the bases of the trunks.

Billy passed them all. He passed the houses of Tibbut and MacDowall; the houses of Anderson, the three smokers, and the messenger. He passed some of the houses many times. He passed the recreation ground, dimly lit by the lights and the traffic of the City Road. He passed the school and its deserted fields, the Infant School, and the Primary School, situated at opposite sides of the estate. He passed the betting office and the parade of shops at the end of that street; the fish and chip shop, the Co-op, the butchers, the fruiterers, the hairdressers and the grocers. And identically designed shops on other corners of other streets. All shut, their windows darkened; daytime reference points about the maze of the estate.

There were few people about; an odd couple, a man, a woman, none of them speaking, all hurrying somewhere heads down. A car went by, tyres swishing on the wet road, a shadow at the wheel. Winking as it turned right further on.

A shadow rippling across a drawn curtain. A light going on. A light going off. A laugh. A shout. A name. A television on too loud, throwing the dialogue out into the garden. A record, a radio playing; occasional sounds on quiet streets.

Until finally he came out into the City Road. It was brighter here and the traffic was heavy. The cars shone in the rain, and their tops caught the colours of the street lamps as they passed beneath them, leaving them behind as shimmering columns in the wet asphalt. Billy stood watching the traffic, turning his head left, or right to follow any vehicle that took his fancy. Then he turned right and set off towards the City. He waited for a gap in the traffic, then walked diagonally across the road, making a car poop, and slow down for him, and the driver look out at him as he reached the kerb. He passed Porter's shop. Hanging on the glass door was the notice, CLOSED EVEN FOR THE SALE OF BRISTOL.

Houses and shops. Flats above shops. A new public house centred on its own car park. Old public houses, terraced, and at street ends. A garage. A tin chapel. A children's playground, the gates locked, behind the railings the paddling pool still

155

drained from the winter. A row of derelict houses, and next to them, standing back from the road, a derelict cinema. Billy glanced at it as he passed, then stopped, and turned back, and stood before it.

THE PALACE. The arabesque lettering still visible in the plaster above the doorway. The architecture of the façade of Graeco-Arabian inspiration. The doorway was crescent-shaped, the supposed entrance to a cave, and directly above it the crown of the façade described the same curve. At either side pillars had been superimposed on to the wall, and rose to turrets flanking the crown. The whole façade had been finished in plaster, the pillars fluted, but these, like other areas of the façade were peeling, revealing the same brick foundation. The Forthcoming Attractions board advertised nothing. An expanding gate barred the entrance, but failed to cover the upper curve of the doorway, and in the foyer behind the gate lay half bricks and stones, which had been lobbed over at the boarded doors and paybox.

Billy slowly crossed the forecourt to the gate. He shook it, and looked round quickly at the rattle it made. He walked to one corner and looked down the side. Behind the façade the rest of the building was a brick oblong. He walked down the side. Near the front a small window had been boarded up. At the back the emergency doors were boarded, and approaching the front again, another barred window, corresponding to the one on the other side. Billy reached up. He could just touch the bottom board; the top one with a jump. He looked around, then scrounged around the building, and behind the row of empty houses for whole bricks, stacking them cross-ways on top of each other, until they were high enough to bring his shoulders level with the window sill. There were two boards across the window. He inched his fingers between them and pulled at the bottom one. It cracked down the centre, opening like a shutter on the nails which held the ends in position, and throwing Billy backwards, dragging a brick down, clatter, with him. He ran down the side at the noise, and looked back from round the corner. The traffic continued to go by. Then a man. More traffic, and a boy.

He walked back up to the window, reconstructed his platform, and removed the second board, snapping it across the centre like the first one. The window was one foot square, covered by a sheet of zinc gauze. Billy pressed it. There was no glass, and no cross pieces behind. He got down, lifted one of the bricks, and punched a hole straight through the square with it. The catch was easy, and the window opened stiffly back against the broken boards. He stuck his head in. A black square. He found the box of matches in his pocket, struck one, and illuminated the square. But his head couldn't follow the match far enough in to look round, so he dropped the match and studied the dimensions of the frame.

Then, right arm through, hooking on to the upper wall inside and pulling his head through; shuffling upwards and sideways to make a space for his left arm. Left arm through, body rotating, head down, stomach pressing into the sill. Half-way through, hanging over the sill like a sack of potatoes. Hands on the sink, pulling. Feet in the air, kicking. Hands off the sink, sliding down the sill on his legs, halted by his feet hooking on to the sill. Pushing off the sill, hands on the floor, stomach on the sink, forward roll, shins on the sink, and stand up.

His breath was loud in the dark. He struck a match. A moment while it flared, then two urinals, a toilet in a doorless cubicle, and the sink without a tap. Two steps up to the door, then the match had to be dropped. He opened the door and struck another. Too dim. He bent and peered about the floor; found a sheet of newspaper, twisted it into a torch, and lit it from a fresh match.

The foyer: opposite him, at the far side, the corresponding door and balcony stairs. The front doors barred, a bare confectionery counter facing them. Around the walls, empty glass frames, and on both sides of the counter double doors leading into the stalls. Billy approached the doors on his side; two portholes, and between them the same metal disc which split down the centre when the doors were pushed open. He lit another torch and pushed one door, edged inside, and stopped it swinging back with his right hand.

The air was damp and reeked of cat piss. The two partitions

were still in place across the back, but when he stepped between them there was no back row at the other side. There were no rows at all, just bare boards sloping down to the front. Where the carpet had covered the centre aisle the boards were lighter, and Billy slowly followed this path down to the front. Sheets of packing paper littered the floor. A few seat cushions and backs had been thrown into a pile against one wall. His torch illuminated sections of the walls as he passed, the once pastel shades of the stippled emulsion now filthy; the vast oblong designs, oblong within oblong, now barely visible; invisible above the radiator spaces, where the heat had blackened the walls in tall smears. At the front the bare wooden stage, and behind it the brick wall. Billy turned round and walked back up the slope, holding his torch up to the balcony. But it was too far, and the light died away in flickers and shadows. He approached the seats piled against the wall. Their plush covers were ripped, and some of them had their fillings hanging out. Billy kicked one of the cushions, then dragged it up to the back. He shoved it up against the partition and sat on it, his back resting against the wood. The torch burned down. He threw it away and allowed it to burn out at his side.

Black. The silence ringing, intensified by the faint hum of distant traffic. Billy shivered and pulled his jacket about him, trying to fold his arms inside it, his hands in his armpits finding the warmth there. The warmth there ... the warmth of the pictures ... the pictures full.... Billy between his dad and another man, tiny between them, down in his seat, his head just showing over the back of his seat. People all around. A bag of sweets down between his thighs. Smoky warmth, cones of smoke caught in the projection beams. Whispering questions up to his dad; his dad leaning down to answer them. Chewing his sweets. Little picture. News, trailers and adverts. Lights going up. Billy sitting up, kneeling up and looking round, waving to a boy he knows. Telling his dad that it's a boy he knows. An ice cream. An ice cream for his dad. Two tubs. Lights going down, staining the draperies pink, through mauve to purple. Settling down, a full tub, and some sweets still left in his bag. Settling down, warm between his dad and the other man. The

Big Picture. The Big Picture. The End. Holding on to his dad's jacket in the crowd up the aisle and in the foyer. Then walking home, talking, questioning. Down the avenue. Then his dad not talking, not answering questions but hurrying. Billy running to keep up with him. What's a matter dad? What you running for? Uncle Mick's car outside. Jud inside it playing at the wheel. Stop here Billy. Jud driving like mad. His dad down the path, Billy after him, catching him through the kitchen door. Light flicking on in the living-room. His mother and Uncle Mick jumping up off the settee, staring and flushed. A trilby on the table. The flesh under his Uncle Mick's eye splitting as easily as a tangerine. The blood streaming out. Screaming. Shouting. His Uncle Mick standing dabbing at the blood with his fingers, looking at his fingers as though he doesn't recognize the stuff on them. Jud coming in. Uncle Mick leaving. The trilby still on the table. In bed. The shouting coming up through the boards. Billy crying in the dark. Jud listening. Shouting. Shouting, louder as the hall door is opened, then footsteps up the stairs, in the front bedroom, no shouting. Moving about in there. Footsteps on the landing. Billy running to the door. His dad on the landing with a case. Where you goin', dad? Go back to bed, Billy. Where you goin'? I'll not be long. Jud behind him. He's leavin' home. He's not! He's not! Hey up, who's tha think thar shouting at? The Pictures. Warm. Full. Smoky. Big Picture. Billy as hero. Billy on the screen. Big Billy. Kes on his arm. Big Kes. Close up. Technicolor. Looking round, looking down on them all, fierce-eyed. Audience murmuring, Billy in the audience, looking round at them all, proud. Billy and Kes on Moor Edge, moor stretching away, empty moor. Billy casting Kes off, flying low, one rapid wide circuit, then gaining height, ringing up, hovering and sliding sideways a few yards, then ringing up to her pitch and waiting on while Billy walks forward. Jud breaks from cover, running hard through the heather. Kes sees him and stoops, breathtaking stoop, audience gasps. Too fast! Must be too fast! Picture blurring! No contact. Jud still running. Kes stooping! Fading, no contact, no contact. Back to Billy on the screen. Back to Kes on the screen. Billy proud in the audience. Casting her off again. Ringing up. Perfectly clear. Leisurely hovering, and gaining height. Waiting on, all clear. Jud breaking. Still clear. Faster, breathtaking, blurring, blurring and fading. No contact! No contact!

Billy jumped up and blundered his way between the partitions, banged through the double doors and felt up the wall for the toilet door. It was lighter in the toilet. The open window made objects just visible. He climbed into the sink, squeezed out of the window feet first, then ran across the forecourt on to the pavement.

The traffic was still running. A woman on the opposite pavement looked across at him as she walked by. He looked round at the Palace, then turned away from it and shuddered. Somebody walking over his grave.

It had stopped raining. The clouds were breaking up and stars showed in the spaces between them. Billy stood for a while glancing up and down the City Road, then he started to walk back the way he had come.

When he arrived home there was no one in. He buried the hawk in the field just behind the shed; went in, and went to bed.